Egyptian Goddess Shifters

MARISA CHENERY

CONTENTS

BAST'S PERFUME

Trapped in the immortal realm by a vengeful demon, Bast is finally freed when a human opens the ancient jar that binds her. He is no ordinary human. He is her mate, a fact Bast tends to conceal — for her time in the mortal world is limited.

When a cat inexplicably appears the moment he opens the perfumed jar, Slade is bemused — then stunned when it morphs into a stunning goddess. Their attraction is immediate, their passion unstoppable. With each blazing sexual encounter, Slade's in danger of losing his heart, but he could lose far more, for the demon is near, drawn ever closer by the lure of Bast's perfume…

CHAPTER ONE

"Let's see what Frank has sent this time," Slade Nelson said out loud to himself, alone inside his antique store, which was closed for the day. With a crowbar in hand, he bent down to open the crate that sat on the floor in front of him.

He and his partner, Frank Thompson, owned a fairly successful store in the middle of downtown Toronto. The partnership worked out well for both. Frank, always the wanderer of the two, traveled all over the world, acquiring items for the store while Slade stayed in Canada to take care of the business end of things. Something he liked doing a lot.

As Slade worked to open the crate, he felt the familiar excitement and curiosity rise over what could be inside. His business partner had gone to Egypt a couple weeks before. The crate, which had been sent from that country, had arrived shortly before he'd closed the store.

The lid now removed, Slade pulled out handfuls of packing material until he reached the items inside. He smiled as he lifted the first clay jar out of the crate. There were four in total, all different sizes, from as large as a wine decanter to a small one not much taller than the width of his hand. The first three jars appeared to be the real thing, not from ancient Egyptian times, of course, but antiques nonetheless. The fourth one gave Slade pause.

This jar was the smallest. He picked it up and held it in front of him as he peered at the images painted on the body. His brows drew together as he studied it closer. The colors of the paint seemed too bright, too pristine, for this jar to be considered an antique. He shook his head. Slade couldn't see Frank making such a mistake. Part of the reason Slade didn't complain about Frank doing most of the purchasing was the fact that Frank had an eye for antiques. His business partner could practically sniff them out from a mile away.

Slade traced one of the images on the jar. It depicted a woman with the head of a cat, a domestic cat. He knew a little bit about the Egyptian gods so he recognized it as the goddess Bast. Next to the cat-headed woman stood the image of a woman who didn't have any animal-like depictions. Slade figured both had to be Bast, in her human and cat-headed forms, since the women wore the same tight-fitting sheath dress. There was no question in his mind that the jar had to be a copy of a much older original. Everything about it seemed too new.

Curious to see what the jar might have held at one time, Slade lifted the lid—and the most intoxicating perfume he'd ever smelled surrounded him. He took a deep breath. Though it had nothing inside it, the leftover scent went straight to his head. The scent smelled so feminine, so alluring, his body responded. His cock jerked inside his slacks as he thought of what it'd be like to make love to a woman who wore this perfume.

Slade snorted. He had to get a grip on himself. He wasn't *that* hard up. At least he didn't think he was. That just the smell of a woman's perfume would give him a hard-on was pretty pathetic. At thirty years old, he should be way past that stage. Unable to help himself, he inhaled more of the scent.

The sound of a meow suddenly drew his attention to the store's front. A black cat stood by the door, watching him.

Wondering how it could have gotten into the store without his knowledge, Slade replaced the lid on the jar before carefully putting it on the counter next to the others. He turned back to the cat, intending to send it on its way, but it no longer stood by the front door.

Just what he needed at the end of the day. To have to hunt down a stray cat that had somehow managed to get loose in the store didn't thrill him, to say the least.

In the end, he searched the entire place twice, but couldn't find it anywhere. Too tired after the long day to work his brain around this mystery, Slade decided to head home. Tomorrow he'd have to see if he could find where the cat had managed to slip inside and block it so it wouldn't be able to return. If he wasn't careful, he'd have mice or some other kind of pest inside the store.

On the way out, Slade grabbed the perfume jar. Since it couldn't be sold, he decided he wanted it for himself. The overall design appealed to him. It didn't have anything to do with the fact that he couldn't get enough of the smell of the perfume it once held.

Or so he told himself more than once for good measure.

* * * *

Slade arrived at his brick two-story just as the sun began to set. After he parked his car in the garage, he picked up the perfume jar and then headed inside his empty house. When he'd first bought his three-bedroom detached, he'd thought it'd be the perfect place to start a family. What he hadn't counted on was his inability to find a woman he wanted to marry and start that family with.

He'd dated his fair share of women, but he hadn't been able to find one who'd tolerate his long workdays, or one he actually wanted to spend the rest of his life with. Once he finally did marry, it'd be to a woman he felt he could be with forever. For him, divorce wouldn't be an option.

He placed the jar on the living room coffee table as he fought the urge to lift the lid and once more smell the scent of the heady perfume. Slade shook his head. How pathetic was he? It'd been a while since he'd last had a girlfriend, but it hadn't been *that* long since he'd taken a woman to bed. He shouldn't be getting this turned-on just from perfume. Deliberately, he turned his back on the jar and headed upstairs to change out of his dress shirt and slacks.

Now wearing a comfy pair of jeans and a t-shirt, Slade headed downstairs to the kitchen. He opened the fridge and grabbed some leftover spaghetti. As it heated in the microwave, he found his thoughts drawn back to the jar that sat on his coffee table. Maybe he could get one good sniff in before his food finished heating…

No. He was going to stay in the kitchen and eat his meal no matter how much the thought of smelling the perfume appealed to him.

The microwave beeped behind him. Once he grabbed a fork out of a drawer, Slade took his heated spaghetti to the kitchen table. Before he sat to eat, he poured himself a glass of red wine. Instead of leisurely taking the time to enjoy his food, however, he practically inhaled it as the remembered scent of the perfume made him almost desperate to smell it again. It was as if he'd become addicted and needed his fix.

"Gee, can I sink any lower?" he grumbled.

He finally gave up the fight as he put his plate into the dishwasher and then picked up his glass of wine before heading for the living room. He set the glass on the table before sitting on the couch. Not waiting another minute, he pulled the perfume jar closer and lifted the lid, his eyes closing as he dragged in lungful after lungful of the intoxicating scent.

Slade's eyes snapped open as the sound of a meow reached his ears. He turned his head in the direction of the sound and sucked in a breath. The same black cat that had been in his store now sat in the middle of his living room.

Slowly, so as not to scare it, he put the jar lid on the coffee table and stood. The cat didn't move as he stepped around the table and went to stand in front of it. Instead of running away, it purred as it wove in and out of his legs. Slade reached down to grab it by the scruff of its neck, but it quickly darted out of reach before sauntering back to once more stand in front of him.

He had to blink his eyes to make sure they weren't playing tricks on him as the cat's form wavered and changed.

Unable to look away, Slade watched as a woman took the cat's place. Once the change was complete, the breath he hadn't known he'd been holding left his lungs in a whoosh.

The woman, who now stood a few feet away, had his blood rushing to his cock. It lengthened and grew rock hard as his gaze took in every inch of her. She had long, straight black hair that made his fingers itch to touch, to see if it felt as silky as it looked. Light brown eyes stared back at him as he roamed his gaze over her face, one that would put any supermodel to shame. Slade gazed lower as his mouth went dry. She wore a form-fitting sheath-type dress held up only by two thin straps over her shoulders. The light blue material hugged her curves and was so sheer he could see right through it. His gaze lingered on her full breasts that he suddenly ached to taste.

Before he realized what he was doing, Slade stepped closer, invading her personal space. His heart raced as he breathed at a rapid pace. The same perfumed scent that matched the one in the jar seemed to surround her, drawing him even nearer. His hands fisted at his sides as he fought the urge to yank her to him. He stared at her. She barely reached his shoulder.

She smiled. Slade's cock jerked inside his pants. Lust like he hadn't ever felt for another woman surged through him. All he could think of was how soon he could get her under him, his aching erection between her legs.

He gave his head a shake as he tried to form a coherent thought instead of thinking how good it'd feel to be inside her. "Who...who are you? *What* are you?"

She took a step closer. Slade looked at her breasts where they brushed against his chest. Her nipples had tightened into little buds that begged him to drag his tongue across them. It took all his willpower not to do just that.

"I am Bast. As for what I am, I'm yours." She spoke with a heavy accent.

At her words, his heart tried to beat free of his body. His cock seemed to harden even more as it nestled against her belly. His chest rapidly rose and fell as he drew more of her perfumed scent. He shook as the need to touch her, kiss her, almost overtook him.

"You're Bast? The *Egyptian goddess* Bast?" A part of Slade found that hard to believe, but how else could he explain how she'd been able to shift from a cat to the gorgeous woman who stood before him?

Bast placed a hand on his chest. "I have the feeling you don't believe I'm speaking the truth." She shifted to the side so she could look around him. "My perfume jar sits on your table."

Slade fisted his hands tighter. As Bast moved against him, it took every ounce of restraint he possessed not to pull her to the floor. "*Your* perfume jar?"

He sounded as if he didn't have a brain in his head by repeating everything she said, but Slade counted himself lucky to be able to speak with all his blood flooding into his cock.

7

"Yes, my jar. Now that you have removed the lid, I am able to walk in the mortal realm."

A tremor shook him as Bast placed her other hand on him and ran both along his chest. She explored the contours of his body as she stared at him with her bottom lip between her teeth. His arousal ratcheted up another notch. He didn't know how much more he could take before he finally broke and put his hands all over her.

"So let me get this straight. You're Bast—the Egyptian goddess Bast—and I somehow summoned you when I opened your perfume jar?"

"Yes."

"And you're mine?"

"Yes, as you are mine."

"Mine as in…" Slade let his words trail away as Bast inched a hand down his stomach to the top of his jeans.

"As in yours to take pleasure with."

CHAPTER TWO

B ast ran her finger along the top of the leg coverings the mortal wore. She had told him her name, but he had yet to share his. Not that she minded. There would be plenty of time for her to learn it after they had made love. All that mattered to her was the fact that he was her mate. She had recognized him as such when he had first removed the lid from her jar. Even though he had replaced it seconds later, it had given her enough time to recognize his scent. And a part of her she had long thought dead had awoken, making her feel more alive. Further proof she'd found her mate. Once her gaze had met his, she knew he had been meant for her.

She pressed her body to his and rubbed against his erection. Wetness pooled between her legs as her pussy ached to be filled. His scent, masculine and all his own, only added to her arousal. She had thought he would have at least kissed her by now. It wasn't as if he didn't want her. The feel of his cock nestled against her stomach proved he wanted her very much, but for some reason he held back.

Now that she had taken human form in the mortal

realm, Bast's days were limited. A few at best. That being the case, she would force him to act soon. She had found him, she didn't want to waste what little time remained.

He swallowed audibly. "Pleasure sounds good."

Bast ran her gaze over him. She found his deep blue eyes heavy lidded with arousal. His dark blond hair he wore on the longish side. The ends just touched the collar of his short-sleeved tunic. Shifting her gaze lower, she took in his broad shoulders and muscular chest. She licked her lips as she swept her gaze over the large bulge in his short leg coverings.

Looking him in the face, Bast went on her tiptoes and brushed her lips across his. Her mate was tall, at least six-foot-three, which she liked. "Then what are you waiting for?" she asked in a breathy voice.

Instead of answering her question, he asked one of his own. "Do you make it a habit of sleeping with men who open your jar? You don't even know me."

"No. Only you. Tell me your name. Then we won't be strangers." Bast threaded her fingers through the hair at the back of his neck and pulled his head down as she went on her toes once more. This time she swirled her tongue inside his ear.

He shook as he made a low moan of pleasure. "My name is Slade."

Bast gently nipped the side of his neck. "There. Now we know each other's names. Is there anything else that holds you back from touching me, or do you not want me?" She pressed her lips against the hollow of his throat just above the edge of his tunic.

With a groan, Slade put his arms around her and held her tighter against him. "I want you."

As if he no longer had the will to hold back, Slade claimed her lips in a fiery kiss. He pushed his tongue past them and thoroughly tasted her. Bast moaned with pleasure as he slanted his mouth over hers, deepening the kiss. Desire pulsed through her. No man had ever been able to arouse her to such heights with just a kiss. The taste of him, the feel of him pressed against her, made the ache between her legs intensify. Bast increased the pressure of her lips.

Slade slid his hands down to her bottom. He cupped it, lifting her so he could grind his erection against her sex. Bast tightened her grip on his hair as wetness leaked between her legs. She would have wound them around his waist and rode his cock through his leg coverings, but the tightness of her dress wouldn't allow it.

After lifting her higher, Slade carried her to a long, cushioned piece of furniture. He put her down, lay on his side next to her and threw a leg over hers. He cupped her breast as he trailed his lips along her jaw and down the column of her neck. Bast bunched the material of his tunic in her hands and pulled it up his back. He quickly lifted himself and yanked it over his head. She skimmed her hands over the thick slabs of muscle padding his chest. She trailed her fingers down the ridged muscles of his stomach as she arched up and dragged her tongue across one of his flat nipples. His eyes closed to half-mast as he groaned.

Slade settled on top of Bast as he licked and kissed a path from her neck to the top of her chest. Inching down the cushions, he cupped a breast before he laved her taut nipple through her dress. As he lightly took it between his teeth and bit down, she arched her back for more.

He tried to pull down the top of her dress, but the straps held it in place. Slade ran his hands down her, obviously looking for a way to remove it before he lifted his head. "I need to feel your skin next to mine. How do I take off your dress without ripping it from you?"

Bast smiled and willed her dress off her. Slade's eyes widened for a split second before they grew heavy with arousal once more. They moaned. Wanting to feel his naked skin against her, she willed his leg coverings away.

He sucked in a breath as his cock pressed against her thigh. The feel of it along her skin had her arching and taking her bottom lip between her teeth. Everything about her mate was large. She ached to have him buried deep inside her, but he made no move to enter her. Instead, he shifted lower on her body and thrust a leg between hers.

His tongue flicked across her nipple before he sucked it deep inside his mouth. As he sucked, Slade ran a caressing hand down her side and across her stomach. At her pussy, he dipped a finger between her slick folds.

"You're so wet," he said with a groan. "I need to see if you taste as good as you smell."

Inching even farther down her body, Slade kissed a path across her ribs and to her navel. He swirled his tongue inside before he continued downward. Bast lifted her hips off the cushion as he placed feather-light kisses down the outside of her thigh and back up the inside. She held her breath in anticipation as he kissed higher. The feel of his breath against her sex made her clutch the cushion. Needing more, she fisted her hands in his hair.

"Slade," she panted.

In answer, Slade dragged his tongue along her pussy before he swirled it around her clit. Bast moaned as she rocked her hips against his mouth. Anchoring her hips in place with one hand, he spread her folds with the other and set to work pleasuring her. He stiffened his tongue and jabbed it inside her core. The pleasure mounted as he sucked on her clit. A whimper slipped past her lips and her body coiled even tighter. It wouldn't take much to send her over the edge. Pulling at his hair, desperate to have him inside her, she tried to get him to move higher.

"Slade, please."

With one last swipe of his tongue, he rose above her, the head of his cock pressed against her slick opening. Bast wrapped her legs around his waist as he thrust himself home. Sheathed to the hilt, Slade took her lips in a demanding kiss as he arched back, then pushed his full length inside again. With his thickness buried deep, filling her to capacity, she squeezed her inner walls around his shaft. He pumped his hips faster as he increased their pace. It had been so long since she had let a man inside her body, but nothing compared to the feel of being joined to her mate.

Gripping Slade's shoulders, Bast lifted her hips to meet his thrusts. She angled herself in just the right way so his pelvic bone rubbed her clit. Her release built and built until she finally fell over the edge. She moaned as intense pleasure washed through her. Her inner walls clutched his cock, fisting it tight. Once the last wave hit, he cupped her bottom and pushed into her. He stiffened with the one final thrust. He buried his face in her neck, groaned as his cock pulsed inside her and filled her with his cum.

Bast wrapped her arms around Slade and held him tightly as they fought to catch their breaths. Their bodies still joined, she didn't want to ever move again. Once their breathing evened out, he propped himself up on his elbows. He gently brushed his lips against hers.

His dark blue eyes stared down at her as he followed the contours of her face. "Are you really here or are you just a figment of my imagination? If you're a dream, I don't want to ever wake up."

Bast pushed a lock of hair off his forehead. "I'm really here."

Slade kissed the tip of her nose. "I'm still having a hard time getting my head around this. I never would have thought in a million years that you really existed. Nor did I ever think I'd make love to an Egyptian goddess."

"Oh, I am real. I've just been forgotten."

"I wouldn't say you've been completely forgotten." Slade glanced at the jar that sat on the coffee table. "Not when we have so many reminders of you and the other gods."

Bast focused on her jar. It had long been the bane of her existence. Bound to it, the immortal realm now her prison, she hated that she couldn't free herself. More so now that she had found her mate. How could she leave him? It wouldn't give her the choice, though.

"What's the matter?" Slade asked.

She pasted on a smile as she turned her gaze to him. His brows had drawn together, a concerned expression on his face. She gently ran her fingers along his jaw. Bast made the decision right there not to tell Slade exactly what he meant to her. It would only make him feel their separation more when her stay there ended, but he did need to know about her connection to the jar. She didn't want it to end up in another's hands.

"Do you remember how I said you summoned me when you removed the lid from my perfume jar?"

"Yes."

"The only reason you can summon me this way is because I'm bound to the jar. Only when a mortal removes the lid can I walk in the mortal realm."

"Only then?"

"Yes. Hundreds of years ago, I had a run-in with a demon, a powerful demon. I was unable to defeat him, but in the end I managed to hurt him. In vengeance, he bound me to the jar. I'm unable to come to the mortal realm unless summoned."

"Why would he do that?"

"I am the goddess of protection. It has always been my sacred duty to look out for the mortals of this realm, especially the women and children. I've always felt a connection to mortals because of it. The demon knew I could no longer do my duty if I couldn't come here of my own free will."

Slade ran a finger along her cheek. "Then I guess I'd better make sure I never put the lid back on. That way you can stay here as long as you want."

Bast sadly shook her head. "It doesn't work that way. I will only remain in this realm for three days from the time the lid has been removed."

"And when the time is up?"

"I'll be sent back to the immortal realm, trapped in my prison once again."

"Then I'll just have to open the jar again to bring you back."

"That won't work. The same mortal cannot summon me more than once. Another mortal would have to own my jar and open it."

Slade took her lips in a searing kiss. After he lifted his head, they panted for breath. Her body stirred to life. "Now that I know the connection between you and the jar, I don't like the idea of another coming anywhere near it. It's mine, just as you belong to me."

Bast closed her eyes as she pulled Slade's head down for a kiss. His possessiveness made her heart soar. Even though he didn't know what they meant to each other, a part of him acknowledged her as his mate. Not wanting to think about what she would have to leave behind, she kissed him for all she was worth.

As she sucked on his tongue, his cock lengthened and hardened inside her. The feel and taste of him made a part of her, the part of her soul he had awakened, want to crawl under his skin and never leave. With each touch, each kiss, the connection between them grew stronger. Her body wept for his, aching to join with the one person who made her whole. This time she wanted to control their lovemaking. Bast lifted herself on one elbow and pushed against Slade's chest as she urged him upright. His cock slipped free of her body as he shifted position. She quickly moved to straddle his lap.

She looked down. His cock jutted between them. With the tip of her finger, Bast circled its head before she moved to the shaft and stroked her fingers down his length. Slade moaned as she wrapped her hand around his thickness and slowly pumped. She loved the feel of him. He felt silky and hard at the same time. Arousal built deep inside her pussy. She wanted every inch of his cock to fill her, to stretch her, but she continued to work him up and down. His pleasure was her pleasure as well.

Slade held on to her hips as he tried to urge her higher onto her knees. "I need to be inside you, Bast," he gasped. "Now."

Bast rose. Slade leaned up, cupped her breast and captured her nipple between his lips as she rubbed her pussy against his shaft. She positioned herself over his cock and slowly pushed down. He sucked harder as she sank on him to the hilt. Rocking her hips against his, she took him even deeper.

Setting a slow pace, she rode his shaft. Her inner walls clamped down around him, increasing her pleasure. He released her nipple and let his head fall back against the cushion. He took hold of her hips and urged her to go faster, harder. He thrust into her, matching her strokes. With a moaning purr, Bast's climax overtook her. As her inner walls clutched at his cock, Slade arched into her, lifting her off the couch as he came.

Contented and satiated, Bast fell against Slade's chest. As his arms came around her to hold her close, she closed her eyes. This was where she belonged.

* * * *

Slade looked down at the woman who lay snuggled against his side. It was very late and they were in his bed. After they'd had a second round on the couch, he'd moved them upstairs. They'd already made love twice more. He couldn't seem to get enough of Bast. He put his nose against her dark hair and took a deep breath. The scent of her perfume filled his senses. It was one he'd never forget.

It'd be permanently etched in his brain.

His eyes drooped. Slade forced them open. He didn't want to sleep. Even though Bast slept next to him, he wanted to stay awake as long as he could. He found it hard to shake the feeling that she'd disappear as quickly as she had come.

He still couldn't believe she was real, or how quickly she'd wormed her way under his skin. Not one to believe in love at first sight, Slade couldn't quite discount it either, given how strongly he felt for Bast. *Can I fall in love with her this fast?* Yes, the sex between them could best be described as mind-blowing, but that didn't necessarily mean he'd fallen in love. Fallen in lust, yes, but love? Whether it was love or lust, his feelings for her were new. He didn't want to give her up.

Slade silently snorted. He finally found the woman he thought, if given time, could be the one for him only to eventually lose her in the end. If he could find a way to free Bast from the jar, then maybe they'd have a chance to live happily ever after.

Yeah, right. As if he knew anything about demons and binding spells. It wasn't as if he'd find anything in the Yellow Pages. He highly doubted any of the psychics he'd find there would possess any real powers.

His eyes grew heavier and he let them drift shut. He really did need to sleep. The store wouldn't open itself tomorrow. Unable to fight it any longer, he gave up the battle.

* * * *

The beeping of his clock jolted Slade awake after too few hours of sleep. He groaned as he rubbed his eyes. Thankful today was the start of the weekend and that the store closed early, he turned his head to see if his alarm had disturbed Bast. When he found the spot next to him empty, he stiffened. *Where did she go?* Slade tested the sheets where she'd lain beside him during the night. They were cool to the touch. Bolting upright, he scanned the room only to find she wasn't anywhere.

After jerking on a pair of pajama bottoms, Slade headed downstairs to where the jar still sat on the coffee table. He told himself not to overreact as he pounded down the stairs. At the entrance to the living room, he skidded to a stop. A wave of relief washed over him as he took in the sight that met his eyes. Bast, once again dressed in her sheer, tight blue dress, sat on the couch as she watched television, of all things. Hearing him arrive, she looked away from it and smiled.

Not caring that he'd probably come across as a desperate teenager with his first girlfriend, Slade crossed the room, picked Bast up and kissed her deeply. Once he released her lips, he pulled her into a hard hug.

Bast hugged him back and laughed. "Good morning to you as well, Slade. I must say I like the way you greet me after you have slept."

Slade let her slide down his body as he put her on her feet. He gave her a half smile. "Sorry if I come across a little bit too exuberant this morning. When I woke up and you weren't in bed, I thought maybe you'd returned to the immortal realm. I'll admit I panicked. I really, really don't want you to go."

Bast cupped Slade's cheek. "It's I who should apologize. I only require a couple hours of sleep each night, so I came down here after I awoke. I guess I could have written you a note to tell you where I would be, but I don't think you would be able to read Egyptian hieroglyphs. And I can't read or write your English."

"No, I can't read Egyptian hieroglyphs," Slade said with a chuckle. "I'm surprised you can't read or write English. You speak it so well."

"I have the ability to speak in a new language once I've

heard it spoken, but I still would have to learn how to write it."

Before Slade could say anything in response, his phone rang. Wondering who could be calling him so early in the day, he hurried to the kitchen to answer it. "Hello?"

"Is this Slade Nelson?" The voice on the other end of the line spoke English with the same accented voice as Bast.

"Yes, this is he."

"I'm Detective Barad of the Cairo police."

A chill of unease ran down his spine. "What can I do for you, detective?"

"I'm calling about Frank Thompson."

"What about him?"

"I'm sorry to have to tell you he was found murdered this morning in his hotel room. We could only find your phone number in his personal effects."

Slade had to take a deep breath to steady himself before he could reply. "Frank didn't have any family. I'm as close it as he had."

"You're also his business partner, correct?"

"Yes. We own an antique store here in Toronto. Do you have any idea who could have done this?"

"Not yet, but we're working on a few leads. I understand he sent some items to your store shortly after he arrived in Egypt."

Bast came up behind him and wrapped her arms around his waist. Slade placed his hand over hers. "Yes. He sent me some antique jars. They weren't ancient Egyptian artifacts, if that's what you're wondering." Except for Bast's perfume jar, but he wasn't about to tell the detective that.

"Do you know where he purchased them?"

"I'm not sure. I didn't notice a sales receipt or anything like that in the crate, but to be honest, it didn't arrive until late in the day yesterday so I didn't have much time to really look for one. I'll be going to the store a little later. If you give me a phone number where I can reach you, I'll call you if I find one."

Slade reached for the pen and paper he kept on the counter next to the phone. He quickly wrote down the phone number Detective Barad gave him. After he promised to call the detective back later, he hung up. He let out a puff of breath as he thought about Frank. He also realized he hadn't asked the detective how Frank had died, or what arrangements he needed to make to have Frank's body returned to Canada. He'd have to ask those things when he called back.

Bast came to stand in front of him, a look of concern on her face. "Did something happen?"

He nodded. "The man who sent me your jar was found dead in his hotel room this morning. The Egyptian police think he was murdered. Frank was my business partner, as well as a very good friend."

Slade wanted to punch his fist through a wall. His emotions bounced from anger to sorrow and back to anger again. It was so unfair. Frank was the same age as a he — thirty. His friend had still had a lifetime left. He hoped the police caught whoever killed him and locked the asshole behind bars for the rest of his life.

Bast put her arms around him and hugged him close. "I'm so sorry."

Holding Bast against him, Slade kissed the top of her head. "I have to open the store soon. And I have to see if I can find some information the detective wanted. I don't want to leave you here alone. Would you like to come with me?"

"Of course I want to come." Bast stepped out of the circle of his arms. "I am ready to leave whenever you are."

Slade looked Bast up and down. Her dress was perfect for inside his house, but it revealed all too much of her for outside. The only man allowed to see that much of her delectable body was him. "Um, I really hate to say this, because I do love the way you look in your dress, but you're not stepping outside like that."

Bast looked down at herself. "I'm covered, am I not?"

"Ah, yes and no. Let's just say it isn't appropriate wear for Canada. You need something a little less...see-through."

A smile tugged at Bast's lips. "I understand. I've been watching the box with pictures. I think I know what would be appropriate."

In a blink of an eye, Bast stood dressed in a pair of tight short-shorts and a barely there tank top, which didn't have a bra under it. Slade gulped at the sight. If anything, she looked even hotter in that outfit. It made him wonder what exactly she'd been watching on TV while he'd slept.

"Ah, almost. You could wear this, but then I'd have to beat the crap out of any man who looked your way."

Bast shook her head with a smile. "We can't have that."

"No, we can't."

Remembering the pile of advertisement flyers he'd yet to throw in the recycle bin, Slade took Bast by the hand and led her back to the living room. He pulled the pile of flyers from the open bottom of the coffee table and then flipped through them until he found some that advertised women's clothing. Soon she wore a lightweight, flower-print, sleeveless dress with strappy, low-heeled sandals. She even wore a bra and panties underneath. He knew because she'd willed those onto her first before the dress. The sight of her in only them made Him wish he had time to take her upstairs and make love to her once again.

After Bast did a little spin, Slade nodded. "Perfect. Now I have to go upstairs and change. I won't be a minute."

Before he could head for the stairs, Bast said, "Let me."

His pajama bottoms disappeared. When the seconds ticked by and no clothes appeared on him, Slade looked at Bast. The heated look she gave him made the words he was about to say catch in his throat. He got an instant hard-on. As she licked her lips while staring at his cock, Slade groaned.

"If you keep staring at me like that, we'll never get out of here, Bast."

Her gaze jerked to his face. "I'm sorry. After I willed your pants away I realized I did not know what you wear to your store."

Slade resisted the urge to yank her into his arms and take her to the floor. There would be plenty of time to do that later. "How about I just go upstairs and get dressed the normal way. It'll be less time consuming." Before he could change his mind, he hurried up the stairs to dress.

CHAPTER THREE

S lade saw the drive to his store in a whole new light when seen through Bast's eyes. She ohhed and ahhed at the scenery. Once they reached Bloor Street, where his store was situated, her eyes widened as she took in the busy sights and sounds. As for the car ride itself, she seemed to have no reservations about it right from the time he'd helped her inside.

After parking in front of the store, Slade came around and helped Bast out. He kept his fingers linked with hers as he led her to the front door. Since he wanted time to search the crate before he opened the store, he locked the door behind them once they stepped inside. The crate sat near the counter at the back of the store, where he'd left it.

Bast fingered the three other jars that sat on the counter as Slade dug through the packing material. On the very bottom he found a sheet of paper folded in half. He unfolded it and had to take a deep breath as he stared down at Frank's handwriting. At first, he couldn't bring himself to read what his friend had written, but as Bast came closer and the scent of her perfume swirled around him, he managed to get it together enough to focus.

As he read through Frank's note, he summarized it for Bast. "It looks as if Frank bought your jar and the others from a local market. He also says here that the owner of the small store was quite insistent Frank buy your jar when he found out he planned to ship them to Canada. At first, Frank refused, but when the owner quoted him a price for all four jars he couldn't pass up, he changed his mind."

"Does he give the name of the place where he purchased them?"

Slade nodded. "Yes. He also has the name of the store owner. I'd better call the detective and let him know what I found. Cairo is six hours ahead of us, and I don't want to wait until it's too late in the day over there."

Bast wandered around the store and looked at all the items he had on display as he made the call to Detective Barad. By the end of the conversation, Slade felt as if his stomach were tied in knots. The detective had been very interested in the information Slade had given him. He'd also revealed more facts about Frank's cause of death. Just the thought of what his friend had to have endured during his final moments made Slade feel sick to his stomach. A real chill of fear ran through him as he turned his gaze on Bast.

She walked back to him once he'd hung up. Her brows drew together as her gaze landed on his face. "Something the detective said has unsettled you."

Slade wrapped his arms around Bast's waist and pulled her closer as he gazed at her. "The detective was familiar with the name of the man who sold Frank the jars. He was murdered a day before Frank. Apparently, they died the same way. When their bodies were found, it looked as if someone had hacked them to pieces." He paused for a second before he told her the rest. "The detective said another man was also killed in the same way, and he could be traced back from the man who sold the jars to Frank.

They think this man took something from a temple ruin called Bubastis, which could have led to his death. Before he died, the police think he sold whatever he'd found to the owner of the store, who in turn could have sold it to Frank."

As he spoke, Bast's face grew pallid. She gazed at him with real fear in her eyes. "Bubastis at one time was my city of worship, where mortals came to pay homage to me. After the demon bound me to the jar, he said it would be hidden where no mortal would find it. He must have hidden it somewhere inside my temple."

"Well, it was obviously found by the first man who was murdered or Frank wouldn't have ended up with it."

"He knows it has been found," Bast said softly.

"Who knows?"

"The demon. He knows. He is the one who killed your friend and the other two men. He's following the trail of my jar. He'll hunt you next."

That thought had crossed Slade's mind when he had been on the phone with the detective. If the demon had been behind the killings, and able to track where Bast's jar had gone each time, he'd more than likely be able to trace it the store, or to Slade's home. Slade had no knowledge about demons, but he didn't plan to just sit around and wait for the thing to show up to kill him.

Slade placed his hand under Bast's chin and forced her to look him directly in the eyes. "Now is not the time to panic. You've dealt with this demon before."

"Yes, but he defeated me."

"Tell me about that encounter. Did you fight him hand to hand? Or another way?"

"When he first attacked, he tried to subdue me physically. I escaped his clutches with one of my powers."

"What power?"

"I shot him with a bolt of energy. It didn't kill him, but it did weaken him. Before I could hit him with another, he flashed himself to the demon realm in the underworld."

"Then what happened?"

"He came back. He entrapped me before I became aware of his presence. This time he came prepared with a binding spell. Before I could gather my powers, he'd completed the spell, and I became bound to the perfume jar, unable to either leave my chambers in the immortal realm or walk in the mortal one."

"Can the demon be killed like a mortal?"

"Yes, but you aren't a warrior. You wouldn't be able to defeat him in a fight."

Slade smiled. "I may not be a warrior, but I do have a weapon that will stop him nonetheless. It's called a gun. I don't just collect antiques. I also have a gun collection. As long as the demon isn't bulletproof, I'll be able to take care of him with one of my guns."

Bast shook her head. "It's too risky. Maybe you should try to send me back to the immortal realm. Today. If the demon comes and he thinks you haven't opened my jar, maybe he'll take it and leave you alone. Replacing the lid on the jar should still send me back, even though it has been off for a while now."

"I won't do it. I'm not giving you up any earlier than I have to. And what do you mean you *think* if I replace the lid it will send you back? Don't you know?"

"You are the first mortal to open my jar since the demon bound me. I don't know what will happen if the lid is replaced before my days here are over, now that I have been here almost a day."

"I don't understand. If I'm the first to open your jar, how do you know how long you have here? And that once you leave I can't summon you for a second time?"

"Those stipulations were part of his spell. I guess he felt he needed them in case my jar was ever found."

Slade brushed his lips across hers. "I won't do it. I won't give you up. Not even for a demon. "

Bast shook her head as a look of dread crossed her face. "He will come. Be it today or the next, he will come for my jar. And then you will die."

"We'll figure this out, Bast. For now, I think it best that I close the shop for the day. All my guns are at home. If this demon does show up, I think between your powers and my gun we should be able to take care of him." As Bast began to say something, Slade interrupted. "I know you're afraid, but I'm not going to let the demon spoil the time we have left." She sighed and nodded.

Slade pulled Bast close. Seeing the very real fear she had for the demon did have him worried, more than he'd let on. He was a man. He should be able to protect his woman, but realistically that may not be possible.

Who was he kidding? Bast was an immortal Egyptian goddess, and she'd lost the first time in the end. If it came down to a fight, he hoped he survived long enough to at least keep the demon from taking the jar.

* * * *

As he'd suggested, Slade closed the store. This morning he'd originally thought to take her out to eat before they returned to his house, but on the drive he learned Bast didn't eat. Ever. Nor did she have to drink. That pretty much put a damper on treating her to a nice meal.

At his place, Slade went upstairs to his bedroom to change out of his work clothes. Bast remained downstairs. She'd been awfully quiet since leaving the store. And when he'd said he was going to his room, she'd just nodded and gone into the living room. He'd hoped she'd follow him upstairs. Being with her, with the smell of her intoxicating perfume in his nose, he walked around the majority of the time semi-aroused.

He wanted her again. She was like an addiction. Thoughts of her constantly filled his mind. The very idea of losing her made him feel as if he'd lose a piece of himself. She was everything he wanted in a woman.

Slade changed before he went to his closet. He reached to the very back of the top shelf and pulled out the heavy, fireproof metal lockbox where he kept his guns. The bullets were locked in another one, which he took out as well. After placing both lockboxes on the bed, he went to his dresser and dug around in his underwear drawer for the keys to open them.

He sat on the bed as he unlocked the boxes. After choosing the smaller semi-automatic, he grabbed some bullets and then loaded the gun. With that done, Slade locked both boxes before returning them to the shelf inside his closet and hiding the keys back in his dresser drawer.

Slade returned to the bed and picked up the gun. He pulled back on the slide, then released it to load the first round into the chamber. The gun was now ready to be fired. As he checked to make sure the safety was still on, Bast's arms wound around his chest from behind. He hadn't heard her come upstairs.

He turned his head to the side and looked over his shoulder, where she knelt. "Did you get lonely down there by yourself?"

"Maybe just a little."

Slade shivered as Bast nibbled his earlobe. "Is that so? Well, I can fix that."

Bast shoved her hands up his t-shirt and ran them across his chest. She tugged his nipples before she trailed down across his abs. Slade sat still as she continued downward. He sucked in a breath once she held his cock. He grew hard as she caressed him through his sweat pants. With her every touch, the hold she had over him seemed to grow stronger. She'd become his addiction. Her taste, the feel of her bare skin, the smell of her intoxicating perfume drugged him. Reaching behind him, he cupped the back of her head as he took her lips in a heated kiss.

Their tongues met as he pushed his way inside. She pushed his arousal to even greater heights.

Fully aroused, Slade pulled away from Bast and put the gun on the small bedside table. He turned back to see her watching him through heavy-lidded eyes. Her cheeks were flushed pink with arousal. As he watched, she licked her lips and her gaze slid down to the crotch of his sweatpants.

Slade's heart raced. He still had a hard time believing this beautiful woman, this goddess, was his for the taking. Each time they made love he felt as if she touched a part of him that had never been touched before. She'd become a necessity, something he didn't want to live without. With a jerk, he yanked his t-shirt over his head and then let it drop to the floor before he once again joined Bast.

Slade crowded her until she fell back. He straddled her legs and placed his hands on either side of her head as he held his body above hers. Bast wrapped her hands around his neck and pulled his head down until their lips met. As he nibbled and sucked at her mouth, he worked on the buttons that ran down the front of her dress. This time he wanted to undress her a little bit at a time, and kiss every inch of skin he bared until he could no longer think straight.

Once he had the buttons undone, he settled beside her as he slowly pushed the top of Bast's dress over her shoulders and partway down her arms. Leaving her mouth, Slade nibbled his way down her chin to her collarbone, where he dragged his tongue across her skin. She moaned and tried to lift her arms, but the dress prevented it.

He pressed his lips lower until he reached the top of the pale blue lacey bra that covered her breasts. Bast squirmed as she tried to free her arms. To stop her, he threw one of his legs over hers and shifted so he lay half on top her.

Bast groaned. "I want to touch you, Slade."

"Not yet," he breathed against her skin.

Slade returned his attention to her breasts. With the flat of his tongue, he laved each of her nipples through the lace. Bast's breaths grew choppy as he gently took one of the taut peaks between his teeth and tugged. He moved to the other and did the same before he undid the front clasp of her bra. Parting the lacey material, he swirled his tongue around a nipple, then sucked it deep inside his mouth while he rolled the other between his index finger and thumb. She jerked her hips as she panted.

Aroused almost to the point of pain, Slade ignored the clamoring of his body and pushed the dress down Bast's arms. Now able to lift them, she threaded her fingers through his hair and held him to her breast as he continued to suck on her nipple. He lifted his head as he pushed her dress the rest of the way off. She quickly got rid of her unhooked bra by throwing it to the floor.

Slade watched her face as he glided his hand down her flat stomach to the top of her lace panties. Bast took her bottom lip between her teeth as he stroked a finger along her pussy. He couldn't hold back the moan that escaped him when he found her wet and ready. He hooked her panties in his fingers and pulled them down her legs. She kicked them away.

Bast urged Slade onto his back. "My turn to torture you."

Slade's cock jerked in his pants. "Will I enjoy it?"

She straddled his hips as she pressed her pussy against his erection and smiled. "Most definitely."

Slade soon lost the ability of speech as Bast dragged her nails down his chest. Her lips and tongue soon followed the same path. She pressed kisses across his abs as she inched down his body. He lifted his hips off the mattress when she took hold of the waistband of his sweatpants and yanked them down. Since he hadn't worn any underwear, his cock sprang free. She licked her lips as she pulled his sweats down his legs and off. He gripped the sheets to prevent himself from yanking her into his arms, rolling her onto her back and ramming into her.

Bast moved to straddle his thighs once again. She wrapped her hand around his cock and pumped it up and down. Slade couldn't tear his gaze away as she bent and licked a bead of pre-cum off the head of his shaft. His chest rapidly rose and fell, the sound of his moans filling the room as she circled it with her tongue before she opened her mouth wide to suck him inside. He thought he saw stars appear before his eyes as her lips closed over him.

She kept a firm grip on the base as she sucked more of his cock into the moist confines of her mouth. He lifted his hips off the bed, urging her to take more of his length. Burying his hands in her hair, he held her in place. Bast greedily took as much of him as she could handle.

Slade fought to keep himself from coming. "God, I love the way you suck, but if you don't stop now, this will be over before we've even begun."

Bast swirled her tongue around the tip of his cock one last time before she rose to her knees. With one hand still wrapped around the base, she slowly lowered herself onto it. Slade clenched his jaw for control as her wet inner walls wrapped around him. As she moved, a strangled gasp broke past his lips. His blood roared in his ears. Her breasts bounced as she rode him, her face a mask of pleasure, and her strong muscles squeezed his shaft as he slid in and out of her. Letting his gaze travel down her body, he watched her pussy take the full length of his cock. He grew even harder as he fought to hold back his release.

Bast moved faster, riding him harder. She threw back her head and moaned. Knowing she was close to her own release, Slade circled her clit with his finger. Her pussy clenched around his shaft as she came. Somehow he managed to hold back his climax. He wanted to make her come again before he found his own release.

Before he could roll Bast onto her back, she slipped off

him, moving to her hands and knees next to him. "I want you to take me this way when you come. I want you to take me as your mate."

Slade didn't waste any time as he shifted and knelt between Bast's spread thighs. Bending, he dragged his tongue up her spine as he positioned the head of his cock at her slick opening. With one thrust, he sheathed himself to the hilt. In this position she took more of him, and her passage gripped him like a tight fist. As he pumped his hips, he knew he wouldn't be able to last long. She pushed back as he rammed inside her. Wanting her to come when he did, he reached around and rubbed her clit.

With one hand on her hip as he continued to stimulate her, Slade pumped faster. Sweat ran down his back as he fought not to come, to wait for Bast, but he couldn't hold off much longer. Already his orgasm built. She whimpered and moaned as her strong muscles clutched his shaft and she found her release. It was enough to send him over the edge. Groaning with pleasure, he held her to him as he emptied his cock deep inside her core, giving her everything he had. As he fought to catch his breath, he wrapped his arm around her waist, then moved them both to their sides so he lay spooned against her.

After not getting much sleep the night before, a sense of lethargy washed over Slade. He kissed the back of Bast's neck as he let his eyes drift shut. He just needed a quick nap, then he'd be ready to go again. With a sigh of contentment, he fell asleep.

CHAPTER FOUR

Once again Slade awakened in bed alone. He rolled over and glanced at his alarm clock, then swore under his breath. It was already after five in the afternoon. He'd slept for a hell of a lot longer than an hour. He hadn't expected to sleep that long. It only wasted time he could have spent with Bast. He threw back the covers, got up and gathered his clothes off the floor. Dressed, he picked up the handgun from the bedside table and shoved it into the back of his sweats before heading downstairs.

The smell of something delicious hit him before he reached the bottom of the stairs. Slade followed the smell to the kitchen. Once he arrived, he drew up short. Bast stood by the kitchen table, which had enough food on it to feed an army.

She looked in his direction and gave him a tentative smile. "Good, you're awake. I thought you would be hungry when you woke up. I hope there is enough food."

Slade let his gaze pass over the kitchen table as he walked over to Bast. Roast chicken, a roast of beef, mashed potatoes, three kinds of vegetables and what looked to be both beef and chicken gravy. He seriously doubted he could put a dent in it, even with his big appetite.

He pulled Bast into his arms and kissed her lightly. "It smells delicious, and I *am* hungry. You made this all by yourself while I slept?"

She gave him a sheepish grin. "Not exactly. I used my powers instead of cooking. I've never cooked before. Is that all right?"

Slade smiled. "Of course it's all right. It means a lot that you'd do this, especially when you don't eat."

"Well, I watched the box with pictures again while you slept and I saw a woman making food for her family. I thought I would do the same for you since you're my ma—"

"Since I'm your what?" Slade asked carefully.

Bast pulled out of his arms and shook her head. "Nothing. Why don't you eat before the food grows cold?"

Something Bast had said while they'd been upstairs flitted through Slade's mind. "I don't think it's nothing. Earlier, while we made love, you wanted me to take you as my mate. Is that what you were going to say, Bast? That I'm your mate?"

A look of sadness flashed across her face. "That was a slip on my part. I shouldn't have said it."

"Why? Because it's true?"

Bast sighed. "Yes. You are my mate. I've known it since the first time I appeared to you in my cat form. I didn't want to tell you."

Slade pulled Bast to him again. "Why? Were you afraid I wouldn't feel the same?"

Bast shook her head. "No. Since we are mates, destined to be together, I knew you would feel the same way. I just thought to keep it to myself so when I leave you won't have to hurt any more than you will."

He cupped her face in his hands and forced her to look up. "Whether you told me or not, it wouldn't make my feelings for you any less strong than they already are. I've fallen for you. Hard. Now that you've said we're mates, I know what I'm feeling is love…not just lust. In such a short amount of time, you've become a part of me. I don't want to give you up."

Bast blinked back tears. "I love you as well, Slade. It also makes me afraid. I'm afraid something will happen, that the demon who bound me will come for you. I don't want anything to happen to you."

"Enough talk about me getting hurt. I told you, I have a weapon that will stop the demon in his tracks." Slade pulled out the handgun. "This is a gun. It shoots metal projectiles very, very fast. Since you say the demon can be killed the same as a mortal, one bullet through his heart should end his miserable existence."

"I still think it is too risky." Bast stepped away from him until she stood with her back against the kitchen counter. "I have thought of another way to stop him, but eat first."

Sensing Bast wouldn't say anything more about her plan, Slade loaded up the plate she'd set on the table. While he ate, he couldn't shake the feeling that he wouldn't like this new plan of hers. She looked too sad for it to be anything good.

*

She didn't want her mate to die. The more time Bast spent with Slade, the more she had come to love him. She would rather be trapped in the immortal realm for all eternity than have to deal with the pain his death would cause.

Not knowing if this *gun* Slade had showed her would actually kill the demon, Bast had to convince her mate to try to send her back. If he replaced the lid to do so – since he owned the jar, he had to be the one to do it – she needed to make sure the demon couldn't harm him. She had committed the binding spell to memory hundreds of years ago. She repeated it in her mind as she tried to find a way to break it, anything that would allow another spell to counteract its hold over her.

There was one thing she had thought would be the key to her freedom, but without the jar in her possession, it had been impossible to test.

As Slade ate, Bast went to sit at the kitchen table next to him. It gave her great pleasure to see him eat what she had prepared. She would have liked to share his meal, but her body had no need of food. Being a goddess, as well as immortal, food was unnecessary to sustain her life. Even if she were to gift him with immortality, he would still need to eat, drink and sleep as a mortal since she couldn't grant him godhood.

Bast sat up straighter. *Should I do it?* She hadn't thought about giving Slade immortality until now. If she had been able to stay with him indefinitely, of course she would have no problem asking him for his consent. Given the fact she would leave him so soon after she had found him, Bast hadn't considered it. Now, with a good chance of the demon following her jar to Slade, she could at least do this to keep him safe. The demon wouldn't be able to harm him quite so easily if he was no longer mortal.

Once Slade pushed his empty plate away, Bast stood and held out her hand. He took it, and she led him to the living room and motioned for him to sit. Before she sat next to him, she picked up her jar. She left the lid where it sat on the table.

Slade's gaze flicked to her jar before he looked into her eyes. "Okay, what is this new plan of yours?"

Bast took a deep breath. This would not be easy, but if it worked, it would be worth it, no matter how much she would suffer afterward. "I want you to put the lid back on my jar and then smash it."

Before she had even finished speaking, Slade shook his

head. "No. I told you before, I'm not going to send you back early just on the off chance it'll save my hide. And I sure as hell won't smash that jar. If I do, I'll never have a chance to get you back."

"You must. I think it is the only way to stop the demon. I've gone over the spell he used to bind me. Not until today have I thought to test the one weakness in it. We can use it against him. When he performed the spell, he had to bind a small piece of his spirit to the jar as well. If you smash it, it may be enough to send him back to the underworld. That piece of his spirit will be destroyed along with the jar. It could be enough to keep him from ever being able to return to the mortal realm."

"And if I smash the jar, it may keep you a prisoner forever in your chambers in the immortal realm. Just because it's no more doesn't mean it'll break the spell."

"There is a small chance it will. Either way, it's a chance I'm willing to take."

"It isn't one I will. Say it doesn't send him back to the underworld. He'll still come after me. I know it. You know it."

Bast placed her hand on Slade's thigh. "That's why I want to make you immortal."

Slade searched her face. "You can do that? You can really give me immortality?"

"Yes."

He seemed to think it over, but shook his head again. "No. What good is being immortal if I can't spend eternity with you?"

Bast briefly closed her eyes as she steeled herself for what she had to do next. "I can always *make* you do what I have asked."

"I'll never willingly do it no matter how hard you try to convince me."

"I wouldn't be forcing you with words, Slade."

To show her mate exactly what she meant, Bast looked

deeply into his dark blue eyes. She planted the suggestion that he pick up the lid from her jar. A look of strain settled on Slade's face as he fought against her command. In the end, he found himself holding the lid.

His eyes went hard. "If you love me, you will *never* do that again."

"It is *because* of the love I have for you that I will do it if needs be."

Slade thumped the lid onto the coffee table and slowly stood up. He looked at her as hurt and anger played across his face. "I'll be up in the shower. I can't be around you right now."

Without another word, he turned and headed for the stairs. Bast closed her eyes as a tear ran down her face. Somehow she had to convince Slade to see things her way.

CHAPTER FIVE

Slade stood under the showerhead and let the warm water pound against his chest. Hurt and anger vied with one another. He felt hurt that Bast would actually use her powers to force him to do something he felt so strongly against. He also felt angry that she'd go to such lengths to do what she thought would save him. Wasn't he supposed to be the one to protect *her*? Yes, as an Egyptian goddess, Bast had powers he didn't have...but he still wanted to be the one to look out for her.

His anger drained away as he realized he was acting like a jackass. Just being a man in no way made him able to protect Bast. Since he couldn't shoot energy bolts he knew she could do more than he could with his gun. She'd fought this demon before. She knew what he was capable of more than he did.

Slowly he turned so his back faced the showerhead. Slade closed his eyes and titled his head under the spray of water—then just about jumped out of his skin as a pair of hands ran up his chest. Blinking the water from his eyes, he opened them to find Bast. The sight of her naked body, so close to his, made is cock grow hard. No matter how many times he made love to this woman, she'd always have that effect on him.

Bast smoothed her hands across his chest. "You win. I won't force you, but I need a promise."

To still her movements, he placed his over hers. "And that would be?"

She looked at him, her light brown eyes locking with his dark blue ones. "Promise me that if the demon comes and your gun does not work, you will smash the jar so he can't take it. Please."

Slade didn't want to, but he would promise. The idea of the demon gaining possession of Bast's jar, and what he might do with it, made him cringe. He slowly nodded. "Only as a last resort."

"Only as a last resort." Bast stood on her tiptoes and leaned in until her lips were a mere hairbreadth away. "Make love to me, Slade. I need you inside me."

Closing what little distance remained between them, Slade covered Bast's mouth with his own. He couldn't resist her. He might as well try to stop breathing. His tongue dueled with hers as he ground his erect cock against her. She moaned. With the sound in his ears, he turned and placed her under the spray. He skimmed his hand down her water-slick body. He molded his hands to her bottom and lifted her. She wrapped her legs around his waist so her pussy rested against his cock, her hands gripping his shoulders.

Just like that, intense need pounded through him. No other woman made him ache for her so quickly. Only Bast. The need to claim her, possess her, mark her as his, pounded through him. Slade turned and took the two steps that brought her up against the cool tile of the shower wall. Her eyes were closed, her lips puffy from his kisses. A trickle of water ran down her chest. It collected on the tip of her nipple before it dripped down her stomach. Bending his head, he caught the next bead of liquid with his tongue. She arched as she pressed her breast against his lips.

He took what she offered. He opened his mouth and took her nipple deep inside. As he sucked, he shifted one hand so he could reach between their bodies, brushing two fingers against the opening of her sex. Bast's hips jerked as he pushed one and then a second inside. Her pussy clutched him, and he stroked her, making her moan. His cock grew harder as she tried to ride his digits.

Slade released her breast and removed his fingers. Bast whimpered with need as she rocked her hips against him. Unable to wait any longer, aching to make them one, he fisted his cock in one hand and led it to her wet opening. He gave her only the head as he held her hips in place when she tried to take more.

"I love you, Bast."

Her eyes blinked open. "And I love you, Slade."

With a moan of pleasure, he sheathed himself to the hilt. Hearing Bast say she loved him caused his heart to try to burst out of his chest. Those words were like music to his ears. And those three words were ones he'd never said to another woman. She'd become his world. Another would never take her place in his heart. Pulling back until he was almost free of her body, he rammed back inside her. Slade had thought to take it slow and easy, but as soon as he entered that tight wetness, he couldn't stop himself from pounding into her. She didn't seem to mind. She locked her ankles around his back as she dug her nails into his shoulders. A long moan left her as he slammed into her over and over again.

The sound of their wet bodies as they slapped together filled the shower. Cupping the twin globes of her bottom, Slade increased his pace. His climax built. He angled his hips higher and rubbed his pelvic bone against Bast's clit. With the sound of her whimpers in his ears, he edged even closer to his release. Just as he fell over the precipice, she leaned forward and bit him where his shoulder and neck met. Her inner walls tightly fisted his cock as she came, which in turn extended his climax.

Once he could breathe evenly, Slade let Bast down to her feet. She snuggled against his chest as he reached over and turned off the shower. After he got them both out of the bathtub, he grabbed the thick towel he'd placed on the counter and used it to dry her. He then used it on himself.

Bast moved back into his arms once he was dry. "I'm sorry, Slade. I only thought to do what I thought would keep you safe. Can you—"

Slade placed a finger against her lips. "I know you did. No more apologies. I'm sorry too. I was a little ticked off with you at first, but I know you only did it because you care so much." He put his arm around her shoulders and led her to his bedroom. "Let's get dressed and then go downstairs to watch some television—the box with the moving pictures in it. And let's not allow thoughts of the demon spoil the rest of our night together. Okay?"

Bast gave him a small smile. "Okay. I'd like that."

* * * *

She had to admit it was nice sitting beside Slade on the couch as they snuggled and watched the *television*. He had explained the difference between reality TV and sitcoms. She found she enjoyed the reality TV more than the others that were make believe. And she especially enjoyed show where mortals had to race from one country to another.

As the night wore on, Bast let herself relax little by little. The gun was on the couch next to Slade, well within his reach. Her jar once again sat on the table. She wanted to hope the demon wouldn't come, but deep down inside she knew he would. The big question was *when*. She hated the idea that she and Slade would be caught off guard. The gun may be able to defeat the demon, but if Slade couldn't use the weapon before the demon got the better of him, it wouldn't give him any kind of advantage.

Once it finally grew so late Slade seemed unable to keep his eyes open any longer, Bast decided they needed to go upstairs to bed. She hadn't slept and wouldn't have a problem doing so. This time she would stay in bed even after she awoke. Her final hours in the mortal realm were slowly coming to a close.

Slade's head fell to his chest as his eyes drifted shut. Bast gave him a gentle shake. "I think it's time we went to bed."

His head jerked up as he opened his eyes and gave her a sheepish grin. "I fell asleep, huh?"

She returned his smile. "Only for a few seconds."

"If I go to bed, will you come with me?"

"Yes. I'm feeling a bit tired."

"Good. I want you next to me when I sleep, even if it is only for a couple hours."

Bast opened her mouth to tell Slade she would stay all night right next to him when a cold chill ran down her spine.

She sensed the sudden presence of evil.

Bast stiffened as she frantically searched the room. The chill could only mean one thing—the demon had at last found them.

Slade grabbed the gun and flipped what he called the *safety* off. "Bast, what is it?"

Before she could answer, the demon appeared before them.

At almost seven feet tall, heavy muscled, with long, black hair that fell to his shoulders and dressed in an Egyptian-style linen kilt, at first glance he looked human. Only his red eyes gave him away. That along with the smell of fear and death that surrounded him like an ominous cloud. An uncontrollable shiver of fear ran through her.

The demon immediately backhanded her away from Slade, and she flew to the other end of the couch. Slade lifted the gun in the demon's direction, but the beast swiftly batted it out of his hand before he could pull the trigger.

As the demon's fist slammed into Slade's face, Bast tamped down her fear and she gathered energy to her before she hit the demon with an energy bolt. The demon crashed back onto the table with a roar of rage. His eyes glowed red as he quickly recovered and moved to launch himself at Slade once more.

She prepared to hit him with another energy bolt, but Slade threw himself at the demon.

Both of them hit the floor, with Slade on top. He got in a couple good punches before the demon gained the upper hand and landed another punch on Slade's face. Blood dripped from his nose, and Bast bit back a scream. Afraid she would hit Slade if she threw another bolt, she could only watch as they fought. One of her bolts would instantly kill Slade if she hit him by mistake. It was as if she were living a nightmare.

Moving swiftly to see if she could hit the demon from another angle without endangering Slade, her foot connected with something cold and metallic. She looked down to find the gun at her feet. Slade had shown her how to fire it. She knew all she needed to do was pull the trigger...

Bast's hands shook as she picked up the gun and pointed it in the demon's direction.

With a deep breath, she aimed for the demon's back and squeezed. The gun went off with a loud bang, but the bullet didn't hit its mark. Instead, it buried itself in the floor next to the two combatants.

As she prepared to take a second shot, a large dagger suddenly appeared in the demon's hand—and she cried out as he buried it into Slade's stomach.

With a scream of denial, Bast pulled the trigger again. This time the bullet grazed the demon's arm as he drew back to stab Slade a second time. Slade forgotten, he turned his attention to her. Rising, he stalked closer.

"What do you think to do with that weapon, bitch goddess?" he said with a snarl. His glowing red eyes seemed to bore into her. "You weren't able to defeat me before. Do you actually think you can with that toy?"

"I will not let you kill my mate." Her voice shook with fear.

"Oh, but I will. He took what is rightfully mine. I'll kill him as I killed the others."

As the demon came even closer, Bast aimed the gun toward her perfume jar.

The demon stopped dead in his tracks.

"I may not be able to defeat you, but I'm pretty sure this weapon will be more than enough to destroy the jar."

The demon snarled as his eyes shined a brighter red. "You wouldn't dare." His upper lip pulled back as he growled threateningly. "You destroy the jar, you'll be trapped in the mortal realm forever!"

Bast's heart soared. That was all she had needed to hear.

Without another thought, she squeezed the trigger. This time her aim stayed true. The jar exploded into pieces as the bullet hit dead center.

She turned her attention back to the demon as he roared with rage — and in an instant, he disappeared back to the underworld.

Shaking, Bast flipped the safety on the gun and let it drop to the floor. A small cry slipped past her lips as she rushed to Slade's side. Blood trickled through his hands where he had them pressed to his stomach. His skin looked too pale as he gritted his teeth against the pain he had to be feeling. She went on her knees and lifted his upper body. He hissed through his teeth.

Bast brushed a lock of hair out of his eyes. "Slade, look at me. You have to forget the pain and focus."

Slade turned his head so he could look into her eyes. "You're still here. You destroyed the jar and you're still here."

"Yes. When the jar shattered it sent the demon back to the underworld and trapped me here in the mortal realm."

"You can't return to the immortal realm?"

"No. We can talk about that after." Bast didn't like the amount of blood Slade was losing. She knew she had to hurry before he bled to death. "I can save you if you let me turn you into an immortal, but you have to give your consent." His eyes started to shut. She gave him a shake. "Stay with me! Will you let me give you the gift of immortality?"

"If that means I'll have an eternity with you, then yes."

Bast gave Slade a trembling smile. "I'm afraid you'll never be rid of me now."

Placing her hand on the side of Slade's jaw, she gathered her powers and sent them into him.

Slade gasped as she shot power and energy through every cell of his body. "The pain is going away…"

Bast pulled his hand away from his wound and lifted his tunic. The stab wound had stopped bleeding and sealed itself as if it had never been. She looked at Slade to find him staring up at her in awe. He wrapped his hand around the back of her neck and brought her lips down to his. He kissed her until they were breathless.

After he pulled away, he shifted to his knees. "And for your information, I have no problem being stuck with you for the centuries we'll have together. You're my mate and I'll love you for an eternity."

Bast gave him a teary-eyed smile. "Good, because I'll love you for just as long, my mate. How do you feel?"

"Like I can run a marathon and not get winded. I feel stronger too. I think I can get used to being immortal."

She laughed. "Good, because there is no reversing it."

Slade opened his arms. "Since I seem to have more energy than I had before, how about we see how many times I can make you scream with pleasure before I need to recharge?"

As she threw herself into Slade's arms, the scent of her perfume swirled around them. Now no longer bound to the jar, Bast intended to show her mate how much she loved him every day.

Because it was the love he had for her that had finally set her free.

The End

LOVE'S FIERY ARROW

Aric thinks he's losing his mind when a lioness appears in an alleyway to defend him from some thugs. When she turns into a gorgeous woman, he's even more confused. Before he can even ask her name, though, she disappears.

That night, the gorgeous woman shows up at his apartment and tells him that he's her mate—the man meant to stay with her for all eternity. The passion blazes between them, but they have to make a choice. For them to be together, Aric has to accept immortality, and Menhit must agree to leave her home in the immortal realm, never to return.

CHAPTER ONE

Aric Driscol groaned as he took in the rush hour traffic on Toronto's busy Yonge Street. As a bike courier, the heavy traffic didn't help him do his job any faster. Adjusting the strap of his messenger bag across his chest, Aric slowed his bike. He'd just picked up a delivery, the last one of the day, and wanted to get it over and done with. The package wasn't heavy, but it was long and narrow. The end of the box stuck out the top of his bag and lay against his back.

Thinking there was nothing for it, he changed direction. He'd have to cut through the back alleyways if he wanted to make up some time. While he raced down some smaller side streets, a car pulled up behind his bike and followed him.

At first, he thought the car only happened to be going the same way, but as its front bumper edged closer and closer to his back tire, he started to think otherwise. Picking up speed, Aric decided to try to lose them in the back alleys. He zig-zagged through them, taking short turns, but the car continued following him.

He soon cursed under his breath when he realized he'd

taken a wrong turn. Paying more attention to the car than where he should be going had cost him—he had stupidly trapped himself in a dead-end alley. The car quickly pulled in behind him, blocking his way out. Aric turned his bike around and pushed at the brim of the black bicycle helmet he wore as two tough-looking characters stepped out. They slowly walked toward him. He skipped his gaze over them. The first guy had dark brown hair, which he wore in a buzz cut. He also looked as if he were built like a brick shithouse with fists the size of hams. His partner appeared equally big and wore his reddish-brown hair down to his shoulders. Neither of them looked friendly.

Buzz cut spoke first. "It doesn't look as if you're going anywhere. Why don't you get off your bike so we can get this over?"

"If it's all the same to you, I'd rather stay right where I am." Aric could fight with the best of them, but he didn't stand a chance against those two. He was muscular, though not bulky muscular. He spent too many hours a day on a bicycle to have massive muscles.

Long hair shook his head. "We didn't corner you just to let you go."

Aric had no idea why they'd singled him out. What made him so special? "If it's money you want, I only have five bucks. As for what I have in my bag, I doubt it'd be worth much to you."

"Who says we want your money or the package you have in your bag?" Buzz cut asked, cracking his knuckles.

Had he somehow managed to piss these two off? Aric didn't think he'd cut them off with his bike. Some taxi cab drivers took exception to cyclists weaving in and out of traffic, but he hadn't done much of that today. The only thing he could come up with was maybe they got their jollies from beating the crap out of bike messengers. Either way it didn't look good.

As the two guys stepped closer, the package resting

against Aric's back heated up, warming enough for him to feel the heat seeping through the cardboard of the box and into his black t-shirt, straight through to his skin. It grew so hot he wondered if he'd get singed.

A loud roar of a large cat suddenly filled the area, causing the two thugs and Aric to freeze in place. *What the hell was that?* he thought while searching for the source of the sound. At first, he couldn't see anything, then his heart jumped into his throat as a large lioness stepped from the shadows at the back of the alley. The look of real fear that suddenly appeared on the two thugs' faces would have been comical if he weren't in the same danger of being attacked as they were.

The lioness slinked closer while she curled her upper lip and growled with menace at the two men. She stopped when she drew alongside with Aric and let loose another ear-splitting roar before her body blurred and shifted. Unable to look away, his mouth hung open as the lioness disappeared to be replaced by a woman.

He swallowed audibly as he gazed at her in shock. She had straight black hair that hung past her shoulders. Only able to see her profile, Aric definitely liked what he saw. She had delicate features, a complete contrast to her body, which was slim and muscular. She wore what looked like a kilted skirt that only reached her mid-thigh. Her top, sleeveless and tight, showed a great deal of her midriff. Aric had to wonder if her skin felt as soft as it looked. He gave himself a mental shake. Was he crazy? Right about now, he should be questioning his sanity, not admiring the woman's good looks. He also should he hightailing it out of there, but obviously his flight or fight instinct had completely deserted him.

The woman reached behind her, drawing Aric's gaze to the quiver of arrows she carried on her back. A bow appeared in her other hand as she selected an arrow and then placed it in the bow. The arrowhead burst into flame as she aimed it at the two thugs, who looked as if they were ready to piss their pants.

Aric focused his attention on the two men who'd jerked into motion at the same time. They dashed to their car and then drove away as if the hounds of hell were on their heels. Now alone with the woman, he swung his head back in her direction. When he didn't find her, he quickly searched the alley. She didn't appear to be anywhere. Out of the corner of his eye he spotted something, drawing his attention.

In the spot where he'd last seen the woman, a single arrow lay on the ground. He pushed his bike over to it before he picked it up. *Where could she have gone?* The alley had a dead-end and it wasn't as if he could have missed seeing her leave. She'd simply disappeared. Aric touched the arrow's head with the tip of his finger and quickly jerked it away. The metal still felt hot. Thinking he had to be seeing things, he swung his bag to his front and shoved the arrow inside. Once he had the bag against his back, he hopped onto his bike and continued on his way. He still had his delivery to make. Later he could come to grips with the fact that he'd lost his marbles.

* * * *

Aric reached the corporate high-rise ten minutes later. He locked his mountain bike to a lamppost before he went inside. After he rode the elevator up to the right floor, he pulled the package out of his bag as he approached the reception desk. He smiled at the woman behind it.

"I have a package for a..." Aric stopped and read the name off the package. "For a Mr. Black."

The woman nodded. "Just a sec. I'll let him know. He's been expecting it."

Aric shifted from one foot to the other. He just wanted to get back on his bike and go home. At least Mr. Black didn't keep him waiting. A short, heavyset, middle-aged man soon came out to meet him.

Mr. Black took the package when Aric handed it to him. Before Aric could give him the piece of paper he needed signed to confirm the delivery, the man grabbed a pair of scissors from the reception desk and cut the box open. He reached inside and pulled out a single arrow. Aric shifted nearer and studied it. If he wasn't mistaken, what Mr. Black held matched the one still inside his bag, right down to the fletching. It seemed too much of a coincidence that the woman had possessed the exact same one back there in the alley.

Mr. Black smiled as he noticed Aric's interest. "I see you're admiring my latest acquisition. Beautiful, isn't it? It's purported to have belonged to the Egyptian goddess Menhit, who was a goddess of war. She went ahead of the Egyptian army, bringing down Egypt's enemies with her fiery arrows. With arrows like this one."

Aric swallowed. *Fiery arrows?* The woman in the alley had aimed a fiery arrow at those thugs. It couldn't be. Even if he did believe in those sorts of things, which he didn't, he felt pretty sure a goddess of war wouldn't just suddenly appear in some alley in the middle of downtown Toronto. It seemed too farfetched.

"Interesting." Aric held out the piece of paper Mr. Black needed to sign.

Mr. Black gently put the arrow back inside the box before he took the paper. As he signed, he said, "It is. I've done a lot of research on Menhit, she who massacres."

"Oh." Aric just barely stopped himself from rolling his eyes. Obviously, Mr. Black was the type of person who liked to tell people lots of useless information whether they wanted to hear it or not.

Finally, Mr. Black had signed the paper. Before he gave it back, he said one last thing. "I particularly like that Menhit was a lioness goddess, as most goddesses of war were depicted."

Aric took the paper and shoved it into his bag. As Mr. Black opened his mouth to speak once again, he cut him off before he had a chance to say anything else. "That's all very interesting, but I have another delivery to make."

"Oh yes, of course. I won't hold you up. Thanks for delivering my package unharmed."

With a nod, Aric crossed to the elevators and then pushed the down button. The information Mr. Black had given him about Menhit swirled inside his mind as he rode the elevator to the lobby. He really must have lost it, because at the moment, he couldn't say for sure it hadn't been Menhit in that alley. Too many facts seemed to match—the fiery arrow, and the fact that the woman had first appeared as a lioness. He gave himself a mental shake as he stepped outside and unlocked his bike. He'd go home and have a couple stiff drinks. Maybe then he'd be able to come up with another plausible explanation as to what had happened in the alley.

Once Aric arrived at his apartment building, he hefted his bicycle onto his shoulder and took the elevator to his third-floor, one-bedroom apartment. He left his bike against the wall by the entrance, then turned and locked the door. He ran his hands through his hair once he took off his bike helmet. After a long day of deliveries, Aric was hungry, so he grabbed a yogurt before he took a much needed shower. It'd been a scorcher of a day.

He headed for his bedroom as he pulled off his bag. Aric set it on the floor by his bed and took out the arrow. Still not ready to think about how he had come by it, he put it on the bed. He quickly stripped out of his clothes and then headed for the bathroom.

Feeling human again after his shower, Aric dressed in a dark blue tank top and a pair of khaki shorts. He walked to his small living room and went to the window air-conditioning unit. Cool air blew against him, making him sigh in relief. If not for it, his apartment would be unbearably hot. Satisfied that he wouldn't sweat to death any time soon, he headed to his kitchen, which was even smaller than the living room.

Too tired to cook, Aric grabbed a frozen pasta dinner out of the freezer and then threw it into the microwave. Once he could handle his food without burning himself, he picked it up, grabbed a fork and headed back to the living room. He sat on the couch, propped his legs on the coffee table and switched on the TV.

The combination of food and being outside in the hot sun all day made Aric tired. It was way too early to go to bed, so he pushed back his tiredness and forced himself to focus on the TV. Deciding he needed a beer to round out his meal, he went to the kitchen and grabbed one from the fridge. He sat back on the couch and took a few sips from the cold beer bottle, but all too soon, his eyes started to droop.

Feeling as if he was he could fall asleep at any time, he snapped his eyes open when something warm and furry brush against his shins. As his gaze landed on the lioness that stood between him and the coffee table, Aric jumped. The beer he held dumped on his lap. Cursing as the cold liquid seeped through his shorts to his dick, he lurched to his feet and ran to the kitchen for a dish towel.

As he patted down his shorts, he purposely kept his back to the living room. *I'll turn around and the lioness will be gone. She was just a figment of my imagination.* He threw the beer-soaked towel into the sink and took a deep breath. Aric spun around and once again locked gazes with the lioness that had come up behind him. She looked pretty damn real to him.

※

Menhit slowly walked on silent paws as she kept her

eyes on the mortal's back. She hadn't meant to startle him. When he had started to fall asleep, she'd thought it would be the perfect time to appear before him again. Given his reaction, she now thought she may have made a slight mistake coming in her lioness form.

She sniffed the air around her. Through the strong scent of beer, Menhit easily smelled the mortal's scent. It made her feel things she hadn't felt before. It stirred her body, aroused her, and awakened a part of her that had lain long dead. One look at him and she found herself intrigued. Being an immortal, days tended to flow one into another. That he sparked more than a casual interest from her spoke volumes. A thrill went through her at the prospect of change, of getting to know this man better. She'd had the same reaction back in the alley. To her, her reaction to him screamed mate, which meant this mortal was the one meant for her, her match.

Watching him closely, she stood her ground as he turned around. Their gazes met before she looked him up and down. He wore his brown hair on the shaggy side with the ends of it just reaching the tops of his shoulders. His green eyes stared back at her. Menhit already knew he stood taller than she since he had to be over six feet tall. She skimmed her gaze over him. A loud purr rumbled out of her throat as she took in his muscular build. She couldn't wait to run her hands all over him.

The mortal backed away until he hit the counter behind him. "You can't be real. Seriously. I had to have made you up. I spent too much time in the hot sun today and I have sunstroke. Yeah, that's it. I have sunstroke and I'm out of my head with fever." He placed his palm on his forehead. He frowned. "I don't feel that hot."

Menhit closed the distance between them. To show she was indeed real, she stood on her hind legs and placed her front paws on his shoulders. She ran her raspy tongue along his cheek before she shifted to her human form.

Staying where she stood, she said, "You do not have sunstroke. I'm as real as you are."

His breath left his lungs in a whoosh. "If it isn't sunstroke, then I must have lost my mind."

She smiled. "No, you haven't lost your mind."

"You *can't* be real. Shit like this just doesn't happen."

Menhit took hold of his hand and placed it over her left breast. It automatically molded itself to her. "Do I feel real?"

"Uh, yes." As if he couldn't help himself, he squeezed her breast through her top.

Menhit smiled to herself. "See, I am."

"How...how..."

His voice trailed off as Menhit wrapped her arms around his neck and took the step needed to bring her body up against his. "What is your name?"

"I'm-I'm Aric."

Aric's breath rasped in and out of his lungs. His cock lengthened and thickened against her stomach. She resisted the urge to rub herself against him. Right now Aric looked ready to bolt. "I am Menhit."

"Menhit?"

"Yes. Menhit."

"Holy shit

Aric took her arms from around his neck and stepped out of her embrace before he walked away. Menhit followed him into another room that held a bed and a couple other pieces of furniture. He headed over to the bed and picked up an object. He turned around with one of her arrows, the one she had left behind in the alley. Through his possession of it, she had been able to find Aric, and as long as he kept it with him, she would be able to find him wherever he happened to be in the mortal realm.

He cleared his throat. "You're Menhit? As in, this is your arrow, which is supposed to belong to the Egyptian goddess of war, Menhit?"

She nodded. "Yes. That is my arrow and I left it for you."

Aric's legs seemed to give out when he sat on the edge of the bed. "I must be asleep. This is all a dream. I just need to wake up, and when I do, you'll be gone." He looked a trifle pale, and he shifted away as if she would bite him when she took a step closer.

Menhit caught up his hand. She brought it to her lips and kissed each of his knuckles, even though he stiffened at her touch. "I thought we went through this already. I'm really here." She released him and reached for the ties that held her top together. Slowly she undid it.

"What…what are you doing?"

"I'm taking off my clothes." Aric's heated gaze followed her movements as she slowly loosened the tie. "I want to make love to you. I want you." She looked down at his crotch where his erection strained against the front of his short leggings. "And I can see you want me."

He groaned while she pulled her top over her head and then dropped it to the floor. "Let's just say if I did believe you, which I honestly don't know if I do, I'm mortal. If you truly are an Egyptian goddess, that must mean you're immortal. Isn't there some kind of law or something that says we can't be together?"

Menhit smiled and reached for the top of her kilt. "No, there isn't." She took hold of it and pulled it off. She now stood naked before Aric. Her arrow dropped out of his hand and onto the floor as she came to stand between his legs. She knelt and placed her hands on his thighs. She looked up. His chest rapidly rose and fell while he gazed at her. "I'm yours if you want me, Aric."

He sucked in a deep breath. "I'm dreaming. I have to be. I'm going to close my eyes and when I open them you'll be gone." Aric closed his eyes, then opened them. "Nope, you're still here."

"I'm not a dream." Menhit ran a caressing hand up and

down Aric's thigh. "I know you must find it hard to accept that I am truly a goddess, but how else would you explain my presence here?"

"I could be losing my mind, or the hot sun finally fried my brain."

Menhit laughed sultrily. "I assure you, you are perfectly sane. Don't you want me? Is that why you refuse to believe I'm truly am what I say I am?"

Aric shook his head. "Oh, I want you. Even if you are a figment of my imagination, I want you. I've just never had a goddess proposition me before."

"Then I will be your first."

She inched her hands higher, and taking hold of the bottom of Aric's sleeveless short tunic, she lifted it. With her bottom lip between her teeth, she slowly bared his stomach and chest. Once she couldn't reach any higher, he grabbed the tunic and yanked it over his head. Menhit ran her gaze over his chest and down his stomach. Her mate was muscular, but not overly so. There didn't seem to be an inch of fat on him anywhere. The thought that she had finally found her mate made her shake. She'd waited for so many years for this day. She wouldn't have to be alone anymore. She shifted closer and pressed her lips to his stomach as she skimmed her hands along his chest. His muscles quivered with each light brush of her lips.

With a moan, Aric caught her by the arms and pulled her off her knees. "You're starting to feel pretty damn real to me right about now."

He shifted closer to the edge of the bed. He took hold of her waist and pressed his lips against her skin just below her chest. Menhit held on to his shoulders as Aric kissed and licked a path across her ribs. Her pussy clenched when he kissed higher, licking the underside of one of her breasts. He did the same to the other before he returned his attention to the first.

Her knees grew weak as Aric snaked out his tongue

and circled her nipple. If she weren't already holding on to his shoulders, she would have found herself on her knees once again. He cupped her bottom when he opened his mouth and sucked the taut peak of her nipple inside, sucking on it. Menhit felt the pull all the way to her womb. Her pussy ached to be filled and wetness pooled between her legs.

Leaning her weight against him, she pushed Aric back onto the bed. He released her nipple and inched back until he lay in the center. He reached for her, pulling her down onto his chest. He fisted his hand in her hair as he brought her mouth to his. He slanted against her lips while he pushed his tongue inside and twined with hers. The feel of his hard cock pressing against her belly made her moan. He felt thick and large through his short leg coverings.

Kissing her, Aric rolled her onto her back. He cupped her breast and pinched her nipple while he sucked on her tongue. Menhit opened her legs wider to allow his hips to settle between them. She arched her hips upward and rubbed her pussy against his hard cock. Spasms of pleasure rippled through her, pushing her arousal higher.

Aric trailed his hand down her side to her hip. He released her lips and made a wet path from her mouth to her ear. As he swirled his tongue inside, his hand drifted lower. He shifted so he laid half on and half off her, his fingers dipping between her legs. Menhit purred when they spread the moist folds of her pussy and caressed her clit. He circled it with his thumb before he pushed one and then another finger inside her core.

It felt good to have then moving in and out of her, but Menhit wanted more. She wanted his cock. Pushing the top of the garment he wore on the lower half of his body, she tried to get it down past his hips. Aric pumped his fingers into her twice more, then undid the piece of clothing. With a few hard jerks, he had it pushed down his legs and off.

Menhit looked down Aric's body. His fully erect cock jutted from his body thick and large, just as he had felt through his clothes. She moistened her lips with the tip of her tongue. She couldn't wait to have it deep inside her. Reaching down, she took him in her hand. He jerked as she pumped it up and down his full length.

She wanted to taste him, to take him into her mouth and bring him to the brink of his release, but that would have to wait. She wanted him too much.

Aric pulled her hand off his cock. "No more. You're driving me crazy. I need to be inside you."

She dragged her tongue along his jaw. "Then don't wait any longer. I'm more than ready to have you take me."

Rolling back on top her, Aric settled between her legs. The tip of his shaft probed her wet entrance while he took her lips in a hard kiss. With a moan, Menhit spread her legs wider as he slowly pumped his hips, pushing more of him inside with each thrust. Once he'd sheathed himself to the hilt, she purred with pleasure. He filled her completely. Squeezing down on his thickness with her inner muscles as he rode her, she clutched Aric's back while waves of pleasure shot through her. She lifted her hips off the bed, meeting each of his thrusts.

Aric buried his head in the crook of her neck and moaned, his pace growing faster, harder. Having him move deep inside her, a wave of possessiveness surged through her. He was now hers. The pleasure coursing through her was made more intense by the fact that her mate had claimed her. Her climax built as his hard thrusts pushed her ever closer to release. He cupped her bottom, lifting her so she could take him deeper, and Menhit's orgasm overtook her. With a keening moan, her strong inner walls clutched his cock in a tight fist. His moans soon joined hers as he rammed into her one final time, stiffening above her, and his shaft pulsed while he emptied himself inside her core.

Breathless, Aric collapsed on top her. Menhit wrapped her arms around his back and held him close. He soon rolled to his side, taking her with him. With one leg thrown over his hip, she relaxed against him. Content to just lie next to him, she let her eyes drift shut.

CHAPTER TWO

Not really ready to wake up, Aric stretched. It had to be late given the darkness of his room. The feel of a warm body pressed against his soon brought him fully awake, though. Unable to see much, he looked at the woman beside him. Her long, dark hair lay across his pillows. He reached over and turned on the bedside lamp.

Menhit's eyes were closed, but her brown eyes soon blinked open. She smiled. "You did not sleep very long," she said huskily.

He didn't think he'd ever get tired of hearing her speak in her accented voice. "I guess I woke up to make sure you hadn't disappeared into thin air again," Aric said. "Or to make sure you weren't a spectacular wet dream."

"I plan to stay around for as long as you want me." Menhit lifted the sheets that covered them and settled on top Aric. "I would have thought making love would have convinced you I'm no dream."

"I'm still having a hard time wrapping my poor mortal mind around all this."

He brought his hands up and stroked her bare back. Menhit was beyond gorgeous, especially with her full lips puffy from his kisses. His cock stirred as he traced her straight nose and high cheekbones with his fingertips before he settled back onto her lips. They'd been made for kissing. He moved his hands from her face to her hips and took her mouth in a languid kiss. Once he pulled away, his cock showed more than a little potential.

Aric brushed Menhit's full lower lip with the pad of his thumb. "I'm glad you don't want to leave any time soon. I haven't had my fill of you yet. Plus, I need some more convincing that you're real."

Menhit smiled. "Mmm, I can tell." She wiggled against his hardening cock.

He sucked in a breath. "That felt good. Do it again."

She wiggled once more. "Yes, it does feel good."

He tried to stay focused. He knew where this would lead if he didn't try to slow things down. "We really should talk, Menhit."

"About what?" She gently nipped his chin before she shifted lower, placing kisses across his chest.

"About what?" Aric repeated. With her mouth on him, he found it hard to concentrate. He became fully aroused after she bent her head and circled his flat nipple with the tip of her tongue. "Ah, we should talk about…you and me. About how you came to be in my apartment."

Menhit lifted her eyes, and said, "We can talk about those things in the morning."

Aric sucked in another sharp breath when Menhit reached down and lightly brushed her fingers along the length of his shaft. "I, oh god, I have to work tomorrow morning." He bucked his hips beneath her as she wrapped her fingers around his erection and slowly pumped up and down.

"Then we can talk when you get home from this work."

At this point, Aric pretty much didn't care whether they found time to talk or not. All he could think about was how soon he could bury his aching cock inside her moist heat. As he ground his erection against her, Menhit shifted positions until she straddled his hips. She rubbed her pussy along his length until she'd coated him with wetness. He reached up and cupped her full breasts. She brought him to full arousal so easily. She made him ache for her more than any woman had.

Rising slightly, she positioned the tip of his cock at the entrance of her body and then pushed down, causing Aric to groan as she took all of him. The feel of her wrapped around his shaft made him want to pound inside her, but he let her control their loving this time. She rose until he almost came free of her body only to sheath him to the hilt once again, making him pant.

As she continued to ride his shaft, he moved his hands to her hips. He held her, lifting his off the bed to match her strokes. Even though he'd already come once that day, he another orgasm built. The feel of her inner walls tightly clutching him made him moan with pleasure. Aric looked down to where their bodies were joined. Menhit rode him faster, her hips angled just right to make her moan.

Needing her to come before he did, he rubbed her clit with the tip of his finger. Menhit threw back her head and moaned loudly, increasing her movements. Then she was there. Aric didn't try to hold back his release as her core tightened, fisting his cock. His moans mixed with hers as he came.

Aric pulled Menhit down onto his chest. He tucked her head under his chin and held her tightly. Satiated, he closed his eyes. He needed to sleep. He had to be at work early in the morning, plus lack of it wouldn't do him any favors. She stirred, shifting so she lay cuddled against his side. He kept an arm around her as he turned off the lamp, and then with a contended sigh, fell asleep.

* * * *

Menhit stood in front of the window inside Aric's bedroom and looked outside at the city. This Toronto appeared to be a very large city, and a busy one. She could still see people moving about on the street below, even though dawn was hours away. The mortal realm had changed so much since the last time she had been to it. The mortals' numbers had grown along with their cities. The large size of the population made her feel a bit anxious.

Peering over her shoulder, Menhit looked at Aric. He lay on his back on the bed, quietly snoring. She smiled at the sight of him looking so relaxed. She wanted him again, but he needed his rest. Unlike her, he needed more than a couple hours of sleep a night, especially after the pleasure he had given her.

She turned back and her smile faded. Aric was her mate, and making love to him only made the bond stronger. The need to stay with him, to be with him, had become a living, breathing thing inside her, but she didn't think she could tell him what he meant to her, at least not yet. There were some things she had to think through before she told him. If she chose to accept Aric as her mate, it would greatly affect her. As a mortal, Aric could not live with her in the immoral realm since it wasn't allowed — even if she gifted him with immortality, it still wouldn't be possible because he wouldn't be a god. Menhit didn't know if she was ready to make that kind of commitment at this point. He may be her mate, and she longed to have a life with him, but that didn't mean she could make her decision lightly. She'd never tried to live in the mortal realm for any length of time. She only stayed as long as she needed to defeat Egypt's enemies and then she had returned to her home in the immortal realm.

She stepped to the bed and slipped under the sheets next to Aric. She propped herself on her elbow and studied his face. Part of her powers as a goddess was that she had no trouble seeing in the dark. Just looking at him took her breath away. She had thought she would never find her mate—she had been alone for centuries. Now that she had found him, she never wanted to let him go. She didn't know what to do.

As if Aric sensed her uncertainty, he rolled to his side and threw an arm around her waist, snuggling against her. Menhit settled down beside him, wrapped her arm around his shoulders and kissed the top of his head.

Tomorrow would be another day. Maybe then the decision she had to make would be easier once she and Aric had their talk.

* * * *

Jolted awake by his clock radio, Aric reached over and slammed his fist onto the button to shut it off. He yawned and rubbed the sleep from his eyes. As the sheets rustled next to him, he turned to look at Menhit. The first thing that crossed his mind when his gaze landed on her was how sexy she looked lying beside him with her tousled hair. The next thing was a sense of relief that she hadn't left.

He grinned. "Good morning, sexy. You beat me awake, I see."

Menhit smiled back. "Good morning to you. I've been awake for hours."

"Did I keep you awake? I tend to hog the bed and snore a bit, or so I've been told," he said with a crooked grin.

"No, it wasn't anything you did," she said with a small laugh. "I don't need to sleep as long as mortals. Only a couple hours will refresh me."

"Oh. So you just laid there beside me for the rest of the night?"

"Yes."

"You could have gotten up. You must have been bored out of your skull."

She shook her head. "I didn't mind. I liked watching you sleep."

Aric studied her. Menhit seemed a little withdrawn. Yes, she smiled, and he hoped the night they'd spent together had put it there, but it just didn't seem to reach all the way to her brown eyes.

"Is everything okay, Menhit?"

She leaned in and gave him a light kiss. "Of course everything is fine."

"You look a little down. A little sad."

"Maybe it's because I'll miss you while you work."

Aric grinned, pleased to hear her say that. "I wish I could take you, but I have to spend the next eight hours on a bicycle while I deliver packages."

Menhit waved his words away. "I understand, Aric. Do you want to have that talk you mentioned last night?"

"I wish we could." Aric sat up and looked at his clock radio before he flipped the sheet back. "I have to get some breakfast into me, pack food for the day and then leave for work." He got out of bed and stretched. The feel of Menhit's hand as she caressed his bare ass made him turn back toward the bed. "None of that, now. I really can't be late for work. My boss will have a shit fit if I am. What would you like to eat? I can make you something quick before I leave."

Totally at ease with her nakedness, Menhit slipped out of bed to stand beside him. Aric had to force himself not to caress her body with his gaze while he resisted the urge to throw her onto the bed and take her until she screamed his name with pleasure. After making love to her more than once, he had to finally admit she was no figment of his imagination. He also had to admit his feelings for her were stronger than he would have thought possible. Each time they had made love it'd felt as if they connected on some deeper level.

Menhit shook her head. "I don't need to eat. My body

doesn't require food or water."

"You don't eat? Like ever?"

"Never."

"Okay, I guess that will save me some time then. I'm going to the bathroom and wash up. You can meet me in the kitchen, if you want. I shouldn't be long."

He quickly headed for the bathroom, not waiting for her response. Menhit made too tempting a sight in all her naked glory. After returning to the bedroom and not finding her in it, Aric quickly dressed.

Inside the kitchen, he found Menhit seated at the table lost in thought. He loudly cleared his throat and went to the counter where the blender sat to make a smoothie.

"So what are you going to do while I'm at work?"

Menhit seemed to come back to herself. "I will stay here and wait for you. I'd like to learn more about the mortal realm, though. Much has changed since I last came."

Aric started the blender. Not able to talk over the sound of it without having to yell, he held up his finger for Menhit to give him a minute. He shut it off and, smoothie in hand, went to her side and extended his hand to her.

"I know just the thing to help you learn about the mortal realm. And it'll keep you from getting too bored."

He pulled Menhit to her feet and led her to the living room. He picked up the remote control for the TV and showed it to her.

"This operates the silver box over there," he said. He pointed to the TV where it sat against the wall. "The box is called a television, or TV for short." Aric turned it on.

Menhit stepped closer to it. "It plays moving pictures," she said in awe.

He chuckled. "Yes, and it gets even better." He switched through a couple channels. "With over a hundred channels, you should find lots of things to watch. Now come over here so I can show you how to work the remote."

Menhit soon mastered the remote control. By the time Aric was ready to leave, she'd become totally enthralled with the television. Assured she'd be okay by herself, he gave her a final kiss. After he grabbed his mountain bike, he headed off to work.

* * * *

Aric arrived at the Downtown Bike Messengers' office at exactly eight o'clock. He wheeled his bike into the wide doors at the side of the building and then headed to the dispatch counter for his first delivery. Other bike messengers stood together, talking, while some checked their bikes.

His boss, Wayne, waved Aric over when he saw him. "Hey, Aric. Ready for another busy day?"

"As always."

"Good. Make sure you keep your fluids up. It's going to be another hot and humid day. I can't have one of my messengers out of commission from the heat."

"God forbid. You'd lose out on some money. However would you survive?" Aric asked dramatically with a smile.

Wayne gave him a halfhearted glare. "Ha ha, very funny." He looked down at Aric's bike. "You'd better put some air in that front tire. It looks a little soft."

Aric looked at it, then cursed. He must have a slow leak. He'd just filled it the other day. "Damn. I better see about getting the inner tube replaced."

"Here, let me fill your tire for you, Aric," said Phil, another messenger. He took Aric's bike. "I have to fill mine, too. I don't mind doing yours at the same time."

"Thanks, Phil."

Phil walked Aric's bike to the air pump that hung on the back wall. He and Phil got along well enough, but a slight tension had cropped up between them this past spring. It mostly had to do with the fact that Aric had beaten Phil, the longstanding champion, at the spring Alleycat race.

Turning back to Wayne, Aric lifted his brow in question and nodded in Phil's direction. Wayne shrugged. Everyone knew Phil had been more than a little pissed off when he'd lost. This was the first show of goodwill Phil had shown him since his win. It also made Aric wonder if it had anything to do with the fact that the next Alleycat race would be taking place the following week. Maybe Phil hoped to regain his title this time around, which wouldn't happen if Aric could pull off another win. The illegal race, from checkpoint to checkpoint in rush hour traffic, would land the winner a nice monetary prize. He intended to hold on to his title as long as he could.

Wayne cleared his throat. "Here's your first delivery." He handed Aric a large padded envelope. Before Aric could walk away, he added, "Make sure you fix that tire of yours soon."

"Will do." Aric put the envelope into his bag, then crossed the room to get his bike.

Phil, who'd been crouched next to it, stood. "You're all set," he said.

"Thanks. I owe you one."

"Don't worry about it. Are you ready for the upcoming race?"

Aric nodded. "Yeah, I think so. Let's hope it isn't as humid as it is now."

"That would suck. Well, I'd better let you go."

"Sure," Aric said. "Catch you later."

After adjusting his helmet, Aric pushed his bike outside. He swung his leg over the seat, then headed to the address where he had to make his first delivery. While he rode down the streets, he couldn't help but wonder why Phil had all of a sudden decided to be nice. Aric had tried to alleviate some of the tension between them for the last couple months, but Phil had always brushed him off. Why would he go out of his way to be friendly now? If he won next week's Alleycat race, that would soon change.

He decided to let it go for now as he focused on the street ahead of him. Now was not the time to sustain an injury. He needed to be at a hundred percent if he hoped to be the winner of the race next week.

During one of his breaks, Aric chugged a bottle of water and ate a protein bar. He also thought he'd call Menhit to make sure she hadn't become too bored. Remembering he hadn't explained what a telephone was to her, he paused for a second as he pulled out his cell phone. Luckily he didn't get too many calls on any given day, and he had an answering machine to take any missed ones.

Aric decided to call Menhit anyway. Once the answering machine came on, he could tell her what to do. It came on after the sixth ring.

After the beep, he said, "Menhit, it's me, Aric. Just follow the sound of my voice to the kitchen. Pick up the black thing that's hanging on the wall next to the fridge. Hold it to your ear with the buttons facing you." He heard the phone pick up and then some muffled sounds on the other end. "Can you hear me, Menhit?"

"Aric?" Menhit asked timidly.

"I'm here."

"You are? How did you get inside this black thing?"

Aric chuckled. "I'm not inside it, babe. It's called a telephone. It's how mortals talk with one another when we aren't in the same place at the same time."

"Oh, I saw something like this on the television, but I didn't understand how it worked."

"I should have explained it to you before I left this morning. Are you still okay?"

"Other than that I miss you, yes, I'm okay."

"I miss you too. I only have a couple more hours left, then I'll be home."

"I'll be here waiting."

The mental image of Menhit meeting him at his apartment door with open arms—better yet, naked with open arms—caused his cock to become partially aroused. He quickly pushed that thought away before he got a full-fledged hard-on. Riding a bicycle with an erection wasn't exactly comfortable.

"I promise I'll make it up to you when I get home."

Menhit purred loudly. "And I know exactly what you can do as well."

"Oh yeah? And what would you like me to do?" Aric asked in a husky voice.

"You can give me that part of you that gave me so much pleasure last night. And once won't be enough. I'll want it at least twice. On the bed, on the floor and maybe in the room that has the running waterfall."

Aric swallowed. "That would be the shower." He found he had no problem imaging what Menhit would look like as she stood in the shower with the water running down her naked body. Even better, her in the bathtub filled with bubbles, parts of her playing peek-a-boo, tempting him to join her to see the rest of her. He'd have to stop by a store and pick up some bubble bath on the way home.

Menhit purred again. "We could wash each other's bodies. Then I could go on my knees and—"

He quickly cut her off before she finished that sentence. "Enough, Menhit. You're killing me here." Now fully erect, he had to adjust himself inside his pants. Damn. The first time the woman uses a phone and she already had him worked up. "I have to go before I embarrass myself on a public street by coming in my pants. To hang up the phone, just put it back on the cradle on the wall. Okay?"

She sighed. "All right. I'll do that now."

Aric didn't get a chance to say bye to Menhit before her end went dead. He smiled and shook his head. He'd have to work on her phone etiquette. After he put his cell away, he looked up the location of his next pickup. Setting off to the address, he hoped the rest of the day would fly by. He now couldn't stop thinking about her and all the things he'd do to her once he got home.

* * * *

An hour later, Aric had a near brush with death. Finished with one delivery and on his way to pick up his next, he raced down the traffic-congested street. Actually making good time for a change, he wove in and out to get around parked cars. That was when disaster struck.

One minute he raced down the street and the next he found himself flying over the handlebars of his bike when his rear tire locked up. The car behind him slammed on its brakes, narrowly missing him. A bit dazed, Aric sat and shook his head. If not for his bike helmet, he would have been a goner. After his body had slammed into the asphalt his head had hit the road next. He quickly took stock of himself. Along with the impressive road rash on his left arm, there was a large hole in his pants at his right knee. Blood seeped into the material around it from a large cut.

The guy who'd been driving behind him got out of his car and came to stand in front of him. Traffic drove around them. "Are you okay? It looked as if you hit pretty hard when you landed."

"I'll live," Aric said while he painfully pushed himself to his feet.

He went over to his bike and picked it up. One end of his chain hung loosely from the crank. The other looked to be tangled in the derailleur and freewheel on the back tire. He tried to push the bike to the sidewalk, but the back tire was still locked up solid.

The driver followed him as he lifted the bike and hefted it off the street. "Can I give you a ride somewhere? You're bleeding pretty badly." He pointed to Aric's knee. "And your arm and face don't look any better."

Aric's fingers came away bloody when he touched his fingers to the left side of face. Crap, he really had done a number on himself. Noticing the crowd gathering on the sidewalk to gawk, he nodded. "Sure, if you don't mind, I could use a lift to Downtown Bike Messengers."

"No problem. We can put your bike in the trunk."

Once they had it inside, Aric was about to slip into the passenger seat when he remembered about his bloodstained clothes. Noticing his hesitation, the man pulled an old-looking blanket from the backseat and put it on the passenger side for Aric to sit on. He told the guy the address to Downtown Bike Messengers before he pulled off his bike helmet.

Now that the shock had started to wear off, Aric felt the sting of his scrapes and cuts. To distract himself, he mulled over what had happened. Why had his chain broken like that? He couldn't come up with an answer. It wasn't as if it'd been old and rusty, since he'd only gotten this bike a couple years ago. It didn't make any sense. He'd have to take a really good look at it. Maybe then he'd find what had caused the damage. At least there was a bicycle shop not far from his apartment. He'd have to buy a new chain on the way home. So much for the romantic evening he'd planned to spend with Menhit. Between his wounds, and now having to fix his bike, he doubted he'd be good for anything.

CHAPTER THREE

The two hours before Aric was expected home seemed to pass too slowly for Menhit. She'd long grown bored of television. She had learned quite a bit about this more modern mortal realm, but she could only take so much of sitting in front of the TV. She could have gone to the immortal realm while he worked, but she preferred to stay at his home. If she made the choice to permanently stay with him, she needed to feel comfortable being alone. If she couldn't handle staying there, how would she ever stand being in the outside world? It would take a lot of adjustment on her part, but she would do it for him if she chose to stay as his mate.

With Aric gone, Menhit had done a lot of thinking. She had connected with him, just as she known would happen. The connection, the bond, would only grow stronger the more time they spent with one another. Even now, she felt as if he were slowly becoming a part of her. If she wanted to be honest with herself, she didn't know if she would be strong enough to let him go. For too long she had been alone. Finding her mate was something she had long yearned for, to have that one person who would make her feel complete. She also needed to be with him again, to join her body to his and strengthen their bond.

In anticipation of Aric's return Menhit decided to set the mood for the night. With a wave of her hand, she willed a number of thick candles throughout the living room. Another wave and a large clay bowl and a cloth appeared on the small table near the couch. Inside the bowl, a lotus bloom floated in the water. He would be hot from his day spent outside and intended to wash him with the lotus-scented water. Once she removed the sweat from his body, she would then do what she had spent the day thinking about.

The minutes ticked by, and Menhit worried something had happened. What if the men who had accosted him in that alley had found him again? Even though they had run when she had aimed her fiery arrow at them, they hadn't just decided to single Aric out on a whim. Reading mortals' minds wasn't exactly her strong suit, but she had been able to read enough to know those men had purposely cornered Aric. And that they had meant to do more than try to steal from him. They had planned to do bodily harm to her mate at another's bidding.

The sound of a key being put in the apartment's door brought Menhit back to the present. With a wave of her hand, all the candles in the living room burst into flame before she stepped closer to the door to wait. The smile she had for him soon fell away as Aric pushed it open. The sight of the traces of dried blood on his face, arm and the clothes he wore had her rushing over to him.

"Aric! What happened?" she asked worriedly.

He grimaced and leaned his bike against the wall. "I had a little accident when the chain broke while I was riding my bike."

Menhit noticed the linked metal that hung from the lower part of his bike. "Why did it break?"

Aric shook his head. "I don't know." He slowly walked

to the living room. Once he saw the lighted candles, he turned back. "I know I said I'd make it up to you tonight for leaving you alone, but I don't think I'm in any condition to do it justice. I also have to fix my bike before tomorrow. Sorry."

Menhit helped Aric pull the bag off his back. "You have nothing to be sorry for." She put her arm around his waist and led him to the long, cushioned piece of furniture. "Sit. Let me see what I can do to make you feel better."

As Aric fell onto it, he groaned. "I really should take a shower and wash the scrapes out. I probably have gravel stuck in them."

As Aric shifted and tried to get up again, Menhit put a hand on his chest and gently pushed him back down. "Let me look after you. I'm a goddess, remember? I can heal a mortal's wounds."

Aric leaned back against the cushions. "Then by all means, do your thing."

She picked up the cloth from the table and dipped it into the water. "This may sting a bit, but I have to clean out the wounds before I heal them."

Aric gave her a half-smile. "As long as you kiss it better afterward, I don't mind."

Menhit went to sit beside him, a smile tugging at her lips. "I can do that," she said.

Gently, she pressed the wet cloth to his cheek. He sucked in a breath as she thoroughly cleaned out the wound. Once she finished, Menhit pressed the palm of her hand against his cheek. Her hand warmed as she used her powers to heal the scrape. She removed it and then placed her lips against Aric's now-healed cheek. The only evidence that he had been wounded was the bruise, which she couldn't heal. She trailed her lips across it to his ear.

Aric shivered as she tugged at his earlobe with her teeth. "I don't think I hurt my ear."

"I'm just making sure."

She dipped the cloth back into the water and then wrung it out before she moved to his arm. Same with his cheek, she healed the scrape leaving a bruise in its place. Before she kissed it better, she said in a breathy voice, "Take off your tunic, Aric."

While he did as she'd asked, Menhit willed another bowl of water and cloth next to the first. She dipped the fresh cloth into the second bowl and then squeezed out the excess water before she used it to wash the rest of Aric's face. After rinsing the cloth, she washed his neck and the top of his chest. He watched her, his gaze locked on her lips, his breathing became heavier.

Menhit ran the cloth down his arms and stomach. She bit back a smile when her gaze landed on the noticeable bulge in Aric's pants. Finished, she put it in the second bowl, then went to kneel on the floor in front of him.

"I need you to take off your leg coverings to tend to your knee."

Aric undid them, pushed the material over his hips and gingerly down past his knee before kicking them off. Her pussy clenched at the sight of him, now completely naked, his cock standing up straight from his body. She found everything about her mate to be perfect. Menhit didn't think she would ever get her fill of looking at his well-toned body. The sight of him made her want to lick and kiss every inch of it, which she intended to do very soon. She forced herself to focus on his knee. She would take care of it first before she lavished attention on his manhood and the rest of him.

Using the cloth from the first bowl, she gently washed Aric's injured knee. This one appeared to be deeper than the others. She shook her head over the sight of it. He had to be feeling that one. After her ministrations, all that remained was a large bruise spread across his kneecap. Menhit threw the cloth back into the first bowl and then picked up the second. Still on her knees, she used it to wash his feet, working her way up each of his legs.

Menhit dipped the cloth into the water again before she shifted to kneel between Aric's legs. She ran the cloth along one side of his hip and then the other. He fisted his hands at his sides as he drew in a raspy breath. His cock jerked as she inched the cloth ever closer.

She rinsed it one more time and then gently dragged it down the length of Aric's shaft. His hips bucked as she took a firm grasp of his cock and thoroughly washed every inch of him. Satisfied, she tossed the cloth inside the bowl and gazed up at him. The heated look he gave her in return caused her heart to pound. The expression of longing he wore had wetness pooling between her legs.

With their gazes locked, she licked his cock from base to tip. Aric moaned. "You like that?" she asked huskily.

His eyes dilated with arousal. "God, yes."

Tearing her gaze away, Menhit circled her tongue around the tip of his shaft before she sucked him inside her mouth. Aric's groans filled her ears while she pleasured him, taking as much of him as she could. He fisted his hands in her hair, holding her in place while he rocked his hips against her. She sucked on his cock, making sure her tongue swept the sensitive underside of the head, causing it to grow even harder inside her mouth. Moisture leaked between her legs and down the inside of her thighs. She had as much pleasure from what she was doing as Aric was. She ached to have him buried deep inside her, thrusting in and out.

Once Aric released her hair and pulled at her arms, she let go of his shaft and moved to stand. Aroused, needing to feel him deep inside, now, Menhit willed her kilt and top off her body. Naked, she ran her hands along her stomach and up to her chest. She cupped her breasts and pinched her nipples.

With a groan, Aric grabbed her hips and urged her to straddle his thighs. "If I don't get inside you right this minute, I'm going to explode."

Menhit moved her hands to his shoulders as he dragged his teeth along her nipple before he sucked it inside his mouth. She moaned. "Fill me, Aric."

Sucking at her breast, he cupped her bottom with both hands and shifted her into position. With one thrust, he sheathed himself to the hilt inside her wet pussy. A moan of pleasure pushed past her lips as she slowly rode up and down his thick shaft. He filled her to capacity. With each stroke, the tip of his cock butted up against the entrance to her womb. That he was her mate made their joining so much more pleasurable. And each joining brought them closer together, binding her to him.

Aric released her nipple and dragged his tongue along the side of her neck. "You feel so good, Menhit. I don't know how long I'm going to last," he said with a groan.

"Soon," she panted. "Soon."

Menhit squeezed her inner walls around his shaft while she rode him faster. Her climax edged nearer as she slid up and down his hard length. Aric's hips bucked beneath her, matching her strokes. As she took him harder, she felt the first ripples of pleasure deep inside her pussy. With a sound of pleasure pushing past her lips, an intense orgasm hit her. Her muscles gripped his cock and she spasmed around him. He slammed up into her, almost lifting her off the couch, then he too climaxed. She ground against him as he pulsed deep inside her.

Fighting to regain her breath, Menhit placed her sweaty forehead to Aric's and kissed the tip of his nose. "Did I make you feel better?"

Aric wrapped his arms around her and brushed his lips along hers. "Yes, you did. You can play doctor with me any time." He wiggled his eyebrows.

Menhit giggled. "All right."

He grew serious. "I wish we could stay like this all night, but I really do have to fix my bike. I also want to see if I can figure out why the chain broke. It was perfectly fine. I don't understand it."

She brushed Aric's hair off his forehead. "Do you think someone could have done something to make it break?"

Aric shook his head. "I doubt it. I can't think of anyone I know who would do something like that."

"I don't know, Aric. First the men in the alley and now this."

His brows drew together. "What about the men in the alley? They were just a pair of thugs who thought I may have something worthwhile to steal."

Menhit shook her head. "No, that is not why they cornered you."

"How do you know that?"

"I was able to read their minds a little. They sought you out on purpose to hurt you. I have a feeling they would have beaten you unconsciousness and left you bloody in that alley."

"Why would they have done that? I don't know them. And I think I would have remembered seeing them if they'd shown up at work."

"I don't know. I didn't take the time to dig deeper into their minds to find out, but I do know someone put them up to it."

"You don't think my chain broke by accident, do you?"

"No, I don't. Did anyone touch your bike today?"

"The only person who came near it without me being around was a guy named Phil who I work with. He's a bike messenger as well. He only put air in my tire, and he never left my sight when he did it. The only other option is when I left my bike locked up outside while I made one of my deliveries. Someone could have quite easily messed with the chain while I was gone."

"Are you sure this Phil is trustworthy?"

Aric nodded. "Absolutely. Things may be a little strained between us, but he'd never do anything to my bike. Bike messengers tend to look out for one another. Plus, I've known Phil for years, as long as I've been a messenger."

Menhit gave him a hard stare. "How long is long? Twenty years? Thirty years? That isn't very long."

Aric chuckled. "Maybe to you it isn't, but I'm mortal, remember? I'm twenty-eight, Menhit. I became a bike messenger at twenty-two. So I've only known Phil for six years, and to a mortal, that's a long time."

She grew thoughtful. To her, thirty years was nothing and six years, just a flash in time. It made her think of how quickly Aric would age. She hadn't really thought about it before, but Menhit realized she would have to make her decision to stay as his mate or not very soon. Years could go by before she decided if she wasn't careful.

CHAPTER FOUR

S howered and dressed only in a pair of shorts, Aric set the tools he needed to fix his bike on the floor beside it along with the box that held the new chain. He glanced over his shoulder at Menhit where she sat on the couch watching TV. He ran his gaze over her, stopping at her damp hair. She'd insisted she shower with him and, of course, they did more than wash while in there. Every time they made love, he had a harder time picturing his life without her. He was falling for her too hard and too fast, but he couldn't seem to stop himself. He felt as if she'd been meant for him, which was ridiculous since she was an immortal goddess and he was just a mortal. Could they make things work? He didn't know, but he wasn't ready to give her up, if he ever would be.

Aric squatted and set to work removing the broken chain. His stomach growled, reminding him he needed to eat, but he wanted to get the old chain off first. It still bothered him that it'd broken. In the back of his mind, he kept thinking about what Menhit had said about the two thugs, and that someone had sent them after him. He had to admit it made him a little uneasy to think they'd purposely cornered him to beat him to a bloody pulp because someone asked them to do it.

While he worked, Menhit came up behind him. "Can you fix it?"

"Yeah. I just have to take the old chain off and put on the new one I bought." He pointed to the box beside him.

Menhit opened it. "Where does it go on your bike?"

Aric cursed under his breath as he fought to untangle the broken chain. "It goes around the rear derailleur, then the freewheel, then the crank where the pedals are." He pointed to each part of the bike, saying its name and used his finger to show exactly where the chain would go. With a final tug, he managed to pull the broken chain free. His stomach growled again. He gave Menhit a sheepish look when she lifted a brow in his direction. "Sorry. I'm hungry," he said.

"Then you should eat."

"I will after I get this new chain on."

Aric picked up the old chain and closely examined it. Damned if he could see what had caused it to break. It looked as if it just snapped in half. With disgust, he put it aside and went to reach for the box, but Menhit snatched it away.

"Let me."

"I don't know, Menhit. The chain is greasy, and it takes a bit of work to put it on."

"Who said I would be touching the chain?" A smile spread across Menhit's lips while she focused on it. One second it sat in the box and the next it'd disappeared.

"What happened to the new chain?" Aric asked.

Menhit nodded at his bike. "Look. Did I do it right?" she asked hesitantly.

Aric looked at it. Sure enough, the new chain was on. He smiled and gave Menhit a nod. "Yes. You did it perfectly. I have to say, it's handy having you around."

She waited until he'd gathered his tools before she

spoke again. "Aric, how do you feel about me?" Menhit wore a look of uncertainty on her face as she looked at him.

Aric stood and faced her. Not wanting to touch her with his greasy hands, he rested his forearms on the tops of her shoulders. He took a deep breath and worked up the courage to tell her what she meant to him.

"I like you a lot, Menhit. You're like no other woman I've ever known. I want to be with you, and when I'm not, I can't stop thinking about you. If I had my way, I'd want to keep you," he said lightly.

"And how would you feel if I said I wanted to stay with you forever?" Menhit asked softly with some hesitation in her voice.

"Forever as in marriage and all that?"

"No, not marriage. More like mates," Menhit said quietly.

"Mates? Isn't that the same thing as marriage?"

Menhit sighed. "Not exactly. It's more permanent than your marriage. Mates are forever. When a god or goddess finds their mate, they claim them for eternity."

"Am I your mate, Menhit?" He held himself still, waiting for her to answer. She silently nodded. "How can you be so sure? We've only known each other a couple days. I know we're good together, but that doesn't mean we won't get sick of each other later."

The longest Aric had stayed with one of his girlfriends had been just under a year, and he'd been the one to end the relationship. A bit of a commitment-phobe, the thought of settling down with one woman for the rest of his life usually made him sweat. For some reason, when he thought of Menhit as that woman it didn't freak him out.

She cupped his face. "I knew the instant I smelled you in that alley that you were the one for me. You intrigued me, awoke a part of me that has been dead for so very long. You make me feel whole. After thousands of years of being alone, I have finally found my mate. I know it is different with mortals, and I understand your kind needs time to fall in love."

"Are you..." When his voice broke with emotion, Aric had to stop and clear his throat. "Are you trying to tell me you love me, Menhit?"

"Yes, I love you. We were destined to be together – the bond that has formed between us tells me so. And that being the case, I now have a decision to make. If you think you can't love me as I love you, then I'll return to the immortal realm and let you live out the rest of your mortal life without me."

The idea that Menhit would leave him and he'd never see her again didn't sit too well with Aric. It actually made him feel a bit panicky. "And if I do love you as you love me? What then?"

"Then I will truly make you my mate. I'll give you immortality, which will forge a stronger bond between us. I will have to make my decision before that. If we become mates, I will have to stay here in the mortal realm, because you would not be allowed to live in the immortal one."

Aric turned his head and pressed a kiss to Menhit's palm. She'd just dumped a heavy load on his shoulders. If he found he couldn't love her, he'd lose her. And if he did love her, she'd be forced to give up the life she knew in the immortal realm because of him.

"Can I at least have some time? Some people believe in love at first sight, but I'm not one of them. I've seen too many marriages fail because the couple rushed into it." Seeing the sad look on her face, he placed his hands over hers. "I do have strong feelings for you, Menhit. Stronger than I've ever felt for a woman. Just give me some time to sort them out for myself first. Plus, you have to think about what exactly you'd be giving up to be with me. I'm sure Toronto can't compare to the immortal realm. You'd have to hide what you are if you stay here. Can you handle that?"

"I'm not going to lie and tell you the immortal realm doesn't have its benefits over this one, but what are all the luxuries if I can't share them with you? I'll give you two days. If your answer is no, then I think it best we end things now while it's still early."

Aric groaned. "Can I have three instead? The Alleycat race takes place in three days. It's a bike race all the bike messengers in the city participate in. I won the last one, and I'm already feeling the stress of the upcoming race. I don't want to add to it by having to make such a major decision just before it. Please?"

She nodded. "Three days then."

* * * *

Later that night Aric jolted awake. His heart slammed against his ribs as the last vestiges of a dream, a bad dream really, slowly slipped away. In the darkness, he turned to make sure Menhit still slept at his side. When he saw her in bed next to him, he let out a quiet sigh of relief. He glanced at the clock radio to find he'd only slept for an hour. Rolling to his side, he put an arm around her waist and put his head close to hers. She slept blissfully and murmured in her sleep as he tightened his hold.

Now that he held her close, Aric's heart slowly returned to normal rhythm. The bad dream had seemed so real. In some ways, maybe it had been. Some people said dreams were where the answers to problems could be found that were too hard to face while awake. He had to think they were right.

In his dream, he'd realized too late that he loved Menhit. He'd wanted to tell her that he wanted her to be his mate, but she kept moving farther and farther away the closer he came. He'd shouted her name until his voice had become hoarse, but not once did she turn his way. After she'd disappeared, Aric felt as if a piece of him had been torn away, that he'd never be whole again. The pain of losing her had been worse than anything he'd ever felt. Falling to his knees, he'd bellowed her name. At that point, he'd forced himself to wake up. If this had been his subconscious' way of telling him he already loved her, then he'd gotten the message loud and clear.

Needing to prove to himself that Menhit still wanted him, that she wouldn't suddenly disappear as she had in his dream, Aric pressed against her side. He slowly pulled the sheet down her naked body. She muttered something he didn't understand, but she didn't wake up. His cock stirred to life as he gently traced the outside of her waist and stomach with his hand. Her skin felt as soft as it looked. He didn't think he'd ever get enough of touching her, tasting her. Aric moved higher, cupping her breast, making her nipple bead beneath his palm. His cock jerked as she arched her back slightly, sighing breathily.

Aric pressed his lips to her shoulder, then moved down to her other breast. So as not to wake her, he shifted lower on the mattress. Once he came level with her nipple, he swirled his tongue around the taut peak. Menhit drew in a sharp breath when he sucked her pebbled nipple into his mouth. With his weight supported on one elbow, he caressed down her stomach to the top of her sex. He continued lower until his fingers brushed against her pussy. She moaned. She opened her legs as he stroked her clit, then moved to test the entrance to her body. Finding her already wet, he pushed two fingers into her. He worked them in and out, and she arched her hips and whimpered. His cock now fully erect, he resisted the urge to take her right then. He wanted to taste her first, have her come against his mouth before he lost himself in her moist heat.

Menhit came fully awake when he moved to lie between her legs and kissed a path from her breast to her stomach. "Mmm, what a nice way to be awakened." She moaned as he slipped even lower and laved her clit with the flat of his tongue. "Ohhh, don't stop."

Aric lifted his head and spread the folds of her sex. "I don't intend to stop until you come."

He still found it hard to believe how much he wanted this woman. The need to make them one beat at him, making him ache for her. She was becoming a necessity just as the air he breathed.

Returning to her pussy, he circled her clit with his tongue before he lapped at the entrance to her body. Tasting her, breathing in her scent, Aric wanted to drown in her. She was his everything, he could admit that now.

Menhit moaned and threaded her fingers through his hair, rocking her hips against his mouth. Aric stiffened his tongue and jabbed it inside her pussy. The taste of her made his cock throb. He pushed his fingers inside her and lapped at her clit. The sound of her whimpers rose in volume as he edged her closer to climax.

Once Menhit's pussy clamped down around his fingers, Aric sucked on her clit until the last spasm passed. Unable to wait any longer, he rose between her legs. Instead of taking her on her back he rolled her onto her stomach. With his hands on her hips, he positioned the lower half of her body so she knelt on the mattress with her bottom in the air. He kneeled behind her, took a firm hold of the base of his shaft and led the tip to her wet entrance. He only gave her the head, then pulled completely out of her, teasing her until she tried to push back to take more.

With a hold on her hips, he held her still while he rocked against her, only allowing her to take what he'd given her. Sweat ran down his back as Menhit's moans turned to whimpers. The sound of their heavy breathing filled the room. Still he refused to give her more of his length. Once he gave her all his cock, he wanted her to come again as soon as he entered her fully. He wouldn't last much longer than that. His cock hardened even more with each small thrust. On the very brink of his own orgasm, Aric reached around her and stroked her clit at the same time he slid the tip of his cock in and out of her wet core.

Almost at the point of no return, Aric reared back one final time and plunged deep inside. Menhit cried his name, her pussy fisting his cock while her climax tore through her. It was enough to send him into his own intense orgasm. Digging his fingers into her hips, he held her tightly to him and moaned, filling her with his cum.

Aric pulled out of Menhit and moved her to her side so he lay spooned against her back. He dragged the bedsheet over them. Lifting the hair away from the back of her neck, he placed a kiss there. If the dream hadn't been enough to tell him how he actually felt about her, this joining would have. He wasn't just sleeping with her because he found her attractive. He'd made love to her and used his body to tell her how much she meant to him instead of words. He wanted to tell her right then and there he loved her, that he never wanted to let her go, but he held back. He had three days. When he did tell her on the third day, he intended to do it right. He'd make it a day they'd both remember.

CHAPTER FIVE

Aric and Menhit spent the next two days getting to know each other better. Since it was a weekend and he didn't have to work, they found themselves spending more time in bed making love than they spent out of it. He did take her out into the city a few times, but she usually cut their outings short with a few well-chosen words whispered into his ear.

Menhit's love for Aric grew stronger with each day that went by. She found herself smiling for no reason, happy to be where she was. He had yet to tell her he loved her. He would tell her he loved her hair, her body, but he wouldn't tell her he loved *her*. At first, she thought he would never say the three words she wanted to hear. She then realized he may not have said them yet, but that didn't mean he didn't show her every time they made love. She did remind him once that the third day would be upon them soon. His reply had been that it wasn't the third day yet and for her to be patient.

The day before the Alleycat race, Aric left her alone in the apartment while he ran some errands. Menhit had asked to go with him, but he'd refused to take her along.

He'd kissed her senseless and then slipped out of the apartment before she had a chance to recover let alone remember her own name.

While Aric was out, Menhit decided to take a shower. It was one modern convenience she truly appreciated in this new mortal world. Back in the immortal realm in her chambers, she had a large pool she could change and heat the water with a swipe of her hand. Now that she had come to the conclusion that she was willing to give up the immortal realm for Aric, she would have to learn to fit in. She would be happy living in his apartment—she had learned that was what he called his home—with him at her side. She locked the entrance door, but decided not to put the chain on as he had shown her. She wouldn't be that long, and she figured the one lock would be good enough, not that she expected anyone to try to walk in.

After she washed her hair, Menhit picked up the bar of soap and brought it to her nose. The spicy scent would always remind her of Aric. She finished washing, then towel dried her hair and body. She heard a noise coming from the front of the apartment. She wrapped the towel around her and went to investigate.

She found a man standing in the front entrance near Aric's bike. He'd shut the door, but hadn't pushed it completely closed. Menhit took a closer look at him. She realized he was one of the men from the alleyway, the one with the very short hair. Not only had he broken into the apartment it was also obvious he was up to no good. He reached to take hold of Aric's bike, and she growled low in her throat.

"What do you think you are doing?" she asked with a snarl.

The man swung around toward her. The hard look he wore disappeared when he saw Menhit. His mouth opened and closed like a gasping fish. "You...it's you."

She tried to read his thoughts to find out why he was

there and who had originally sent him along with the other man to hurt Aric, but she ended up getting nothing. The man was so afraid of her that he couldn't keep his thoughts straight. His fear seemed to override everything else he had inside his mind.

Deciding she'd had more than enough of this man interfering with Aric's life, Menhit decided to give him a warning he would soon not forget. She walked closer while she spoke.

"You will stay away from Aric. You can tell whoever sent you that should any harm come to my mate I will hunt him down, along with you and your friend, and rip you apart with my claws and teeth."

Just before she reached the man who stood frozen in fear, Menhit shifted to her lioness form. To push her threat home, she roared, showing off her sharp teeth while she pawed the air with her claws extended. The man let out a whimper and, much to her disgust, wet himself. He yanked open the apartment door before he raced out as if she snapped at his heels.

Menhit shifted back to human form and stepped around the puddle of urine on the floor to shut the door behind him. She shook her head, and with a wave of her hand, the mess disappeared. She didn't think she would have to worry about the man or his friend coming near Aric again. She just wished she could have found out who was behind all this. Aric may not think someone was after him, but he couldn't deny it now.

* * * *

Once Aric returned a short time later, he found Menhit standing outside on the balcony, looking at the city below. He crossed to the sliding glass doors and ten joined her outside.

He put his arm around her waist and pulled her close to

his side. "You left the apartment door unlocked."

Menhit turned to look at him. "I had a visitor while you were gone."

Aric's brows drew together. "A visitor? Who?"

"One of the men who cornered you in the alley."

He stiffened. "What? What happened?"

"I scared him away. He seems to be very afraid of my lioness. He also seemed very interested in your bike. I think if I hadn't stopped him, he would have taken it."

Aric searched Menhit's face. "You think the alley, my broken chain and now this are related." He didn't pose it as a question.

"Yes. I couldn't get anything from his mind, but these aren't random acts. Someone sent this man, just like in the alley. Whoever it is, they mean you harm."

Seeing the concerned expression she wore, Aric pulled Menhit close and kissed her forehead. "I can't think of who could want to hurt me."

"You said you didn't think it could be this Phil you mentioned who you work with, but he was the only one who had been alone with your bike before the chain fell off."

"I'll admit Phil and I have some bad blood between us—I beat him at the last Alleycat race—but I don't think he'd go this far to...to keep me out of this one," Aric said slowly. He shook his head. "No, I can't picture Phil being this underhanded."

Menhit sighed and shook her head. "You may not want to think about him doing something like this, but not everyone is what they seem."

"I know that, but I still can't picture Phil doing it. It isn't as if the Alleycat race is a big prestigious race or anything."

"Maybe not, but maybe it means more to him than it does to you. I think you should confront him about what has happened."

Aric released her and took a step back. "Menhit, I can't just go up to the guy and accuse him of sending some thugs to beat the crap out of me, or about the rest, without some solid proof. If I'm wrong, he'll laugh in my face. At the end of the day, I still have to work with the guy."

Menhit crossed her arms over her chest. "So you are willing to simply wait for the next thing to happen instead of trying to do something to stop it."

"Who is to say anything more will happen? And you said so yourself, you scared off that thug a second time. I doubt he'll be back."

"More than likely, but that doesn't mean others won't be sent."

Aric had to end this conversation now before it turned into a full-blown argument. He didn't want that. Pulling Menhit into his arms, he kissed her soundly. He lifted his head and gazed into her eyes. "I don't want to fight. How about I promise you I'll be more cautious? Without any real proof, I can't do anything more than that."

Menhit wrapped her arms around his waist and put her head against his chest. "I can accept that, but I'm still going to worry for your safety. I would hate for anything to happen to you."

He rubbed Menhit's back. "I'd hate for anything to happen to me as well."

* * * *

The morning of the race dawned bright and sunny with the promise of another scorching hot day. Menhit woke Aric up with a kiss and then sent him off to take a shower. She used the time while he was in the bathroom to polish his helmet that he wore when he rode his bike. Instead of using her powers to do the job, she used a rag she found under the kitchen sink and tap water. His helmet wasn't really dirty and whatever it had been made from already had a certain amount of shine to it. She still did her best to make it look even better.

By the time Aric came out of the shower and joined her in the kitchen, Menhit was putting the final touches on his helmet. He arched a brow in her direction when he saw what she worked on.

"Isn't that my bike helmet?"

She proudly held it out for him to take. "Yes. I decided to polish it for you. All Egypt's soldiers used to polish their helmets before they went off to battle."

Aric took it and chuckled. "I'm not going off to fight. I'm just going to be riding my bike in a race."

"In some ways it could be considered a battle. You have to beat all the other riders."

"That's true." Aric nodded as he turned his helmet to look at it from all angles. "Thanks, babe. It looks great." He gave her a quick kiss.

After putting his helmet on the table, he went to the counter to make his usual breakfast smoothie. While Aric drank it at the kitchen table, they talked about their plans for the day. He thought it best Menhit stayed at his apartment during the time the Alleycat race took place. She started to tell him that she would like to go, but he silenced her with another quick, hard kiss.

"It's not as if you'd really be able to watch me, Menhit. I have to race from one checkpoint to another along the city streets. It's really not a spectator sport. You'd be stuck hanging out with my boss and anyone else at the office during the race. To be honest, I'm not comfortable with the thought of you being alone with them."

Menhit narrowed her eyes. "Why? Are you embarrassed of me?"

Aric quickly pulled her onto his lap and hugged her. "No. No, of course not. It's just Wayne, my boss, can be a bit on the nosy side. He'd drive you nuts, asking you a million questions. You really haven't spent a lot of time in the mortal realm yet. I don't want anyone else to know who and what you are. If you let it slip that you're an Egyptian goddess, other people would think you're a nut case. I'm sorry, but I don't want my mate locked away in a loony bin."

Menhit sucked in a breath. "What did you just call me?"

"Damn," Aric said with a chuckle. "Well, didn't I just mess up my own plans? I wanted to do this right, after the race ended." He grew serious. He locked gazes with her, so she could see all the love he felt for her shining in his eyes. "I guess there's no point waiting now. I love you, Menhit. Even though I've only known you for a few days, I feel as if it's been forever. I can't picture you not being with me. And coming from me, that's a big deal. I never thought I'd be able to settle down with a woman until I met you. I want you to be my mate."

With a cry of joy, Menhit wrapped her arms around the back of Aric's neck and kissed him with all the love she felt. As she pulled away, they were short of breath. "I love you too, Aric. You have made me complete. I have waited thousands of years to find you. They had grown boring and stale without a mate at my side to share them with. When I first saw you in that alley and your scent awakened the part of me that had lain listless for so long, I knew you were destined to be mine. Will you let me give you immortality? You won't have godhood like I have, and you'll still need to eat, drink and sleep as a mortal, but we will have eternity together."

"Yes. I want forever with you. You've made me one happy man, but I still have to ask, are you sure you want to give up your life in the immortal realm?"

Menhit nodded. "This is what I want. I'll only be happy with you, but choosing to live in the mortal realm does not mean I can never return to the immortal one. I can visit if the occasion arises."

"That makes me feel much better to hear that. I'd hate

to be the reason you had to cut all ties with your former life." He unwound her arms from around his neck. "I know I could sit here all day with you like this, but I can't right now. I have a race to win, as a mortal. Now up you go before I'm late."

Menhit slid off his lap. Aric headed for the door. She called his name. "Wait, Aric. I want you to take something with you for luck while you race."

Menhit ran into the bedroom and then picked up off the dresser the arrow she had left for Aric on the first day they had met. She hurried back and held it out. "I want you to put my arrow in your bag."

He took it and put it away. "It isn't going to suddenly burst into flames while I'm riding my bike, is it?" he asked with a chuckle.

"No." She giggled. "I have to will the flames onto my arrows, but as long as you have that with you, I'll be able to 'see' wherever you are. I can follow the race that way."

"Good thinking. Now I really have to go."

Aric gave her a kiss goodbye before he picked up his bike and then walked out the door. Menhit hoped the next five hours went by quickly so they could celebrate the new life they would have together.

* * * *

Even though it was as hot as hell out, Aric found he could keep up the pace he'd set for himself. The race already half over, his times at each checkpoint came closer and closer to Phil's, who had the lead. Aric had a feeling it'd be a close finish at the end.

Hoping to shave off some time, Aric decided to take some shortcuts. As he turned into the first alleyway, thoughts of what had happened the last time he'd taken a shortcut flashed through his mind. At least now he didn't have a car tailing him, but that didn't stop him from looking over his shoulder every once in a while just to be sure.

Aric finally cut across the last alleyway before he had to return to the main street. As he raced between the two buildings, Phil came out of one of the side streets to ride beside him. Thinking Phil had decided to try the same shortcut, Aric leaned lower over his handlebars and put on a burst of speed. He gritted his teeth as Phil managed to keep up.

Aric racked his brain to figure out a way to lose Phil. He didn't see Phil's arm come out until it became too late. With a hard shove, Phil knocked him off balance. Unable to right himself in time, Aric fell over and skidded to a stop with his bike on top him.

Looking up, Aric expected to see Phil way up in front. Instead, Phil turned his bike around and rode back. Aric disentangled himself from his bike and met Phil's gaze.

"Why the hell did you push me?"

Phil got off his bike and carefully put it on the ground. He didn't offer to help Aric up. He stood above him and glared. "You still haven't figured it out?"

"Figured what out?"

"I decided I wasn't going to take a chance on you beating me, so I arranged for a few little 'accidents.' For some reason, my plans backfired. I jimmied your chain the other day. I'd thought if you took a nasty spill that would have put you out of the race, but somehow you only ended up with a few bruises."

Aric slowly stood. Phil had to be a nutcase for telling him his evil plans instead of using this advantage to win the race. He had to have a screw loose. As he shifted his bag on his back, he felt heat soaking through the fabric. He reached inside and wrapped his hand around Menhit's arrow, the source of it. She'd been right about Phil, after all. Man, he hadn't wanted to believe someone he worked with could be so devious.

"You got those two thugs to corner me as well." Aric said it as a statement rather than a question.

"Yes. I paid them good money, and in the end, they screwed up. They babbled about seeing a lioness that shape shifted into a woman or some such nonsense. Even when I sent one of them to steal your bike, he went on about the shape shifting woman being at your apartment. I guess if you want something done right, you have to do it yourself."

Phil advanced on Aric and pulled a thick piece of wood about the length of his forearm out of his messenger bag. Aric slowly backed away. "What are you going to do now? Beat me? You do realize we're in the middle of a race and that the more time you spend here the less likely you'll be able to keep your lead."

"I doubt it. I figure we were so far out in front I can afford to take the time to keep you out of the rest of the race."

As Phil advanced, Aric looked behind Phil and grinned. Phil was going to get a big wake-up call. "I think you're about to learn firsthand what scared the crap out of your hired muscle."

A loud feline roar brought Phil up short. Aric smiled as Phil slowly turned to face Menhit in her lioness form. The look on Phil's face was comical when his eyes went round and his mouth gasped like a fish out of water. Letting the piece of wood drop, Phil slowly circled around her to where he'd left his bike. She snarled as she followed him with her gaze. Before he could hop onto his bike and race away, she lunged for him. Phil went down hard on the pavement on his stomach. She hooked a paw with claws extended into his t-shirt under his shoulder and rolled him over onto his back. She let loose another loud roar, giving Phil a good look at all her sharp teeth. Then, before he could move, she clamped her jaws around his throat. From his angle, Aric saw she didn't draw any blood, but it was enough to have Phil whimpering like a baby. As threats went, Aric had to think hers did a better than average job.

Menhit released Phil's throat and slowly backed away. She snarled her lip at him and growled. With his face completely white, Phil carefully stood with his hands held out in front of him. Not taking his gaze off her, he bent down behind him and reached for his bike. Once he had it upright, he threw a leg over the seat and then took off.

Aric went to Menhit's side and stroked the top of her leonine head. "How did you know to come?"

The lioness' body blurred and Menhit shifted to her human form. She smiled. "You are my mate. I'll always know when you have need of me."

Aric put his arm around her waist and pulled her against his side. "Always nice to know. How about you do your thing and flash us back to the apartment?"

Menhit gave him a confused look. "What about the race?"

He waved her question away. "It doesn't matter anymore. I have you. That's all that matters."

"Are you sure?"

"Yes. I have a feeling my bike messenger days are over."

Menhit reached up and placed her hands on the sides of his face. "Good, because I find I dislike being away from you. Besides, you really don't need to work. I have plenty of riches back in the immortal realm I can bring here to make our lives comfortable."

In a blink of an eye, Aric found himself in his apartment with Menhit. His bike lay on the floor next to him. "I could get used to that. Let me wash up and then I'll give you the present I bought for you."

Menhit tightened her hold. "First, I want to give you one."

Aric sucked in a breath as a sensation of power shot from Menhit's hands and all the way through his body. He gasped. Much like being zapped by lightning, at least that is what he thought it'd feel like, the power coursed through every inch of him. It sank into his very cells. It didn't hurt. It just felt strange. He placed his hands over top hers and held her gaze. He felt as if he could do anything. He felt as if he could take on the world and come out on top. The power moving through him pushed away the tiredness he'd felt from hours of racing. Now, he thought he'd able to ride in two back-to-back Alleycat races and still would be raring to go for another.

Once the power slowly receded, Aric swallowed. "Did you just make me immortal?"

"Yes." Menhit pressed her lips to his. "Now we'll be together forever. We are true mates."

"I'm not so sure the ring I bought you is going to be able to top that gift," he said with a laugh.

Menhit smiled, then flashed their clothes away. She stepped into his arms and brushed up against him. "I'm sure I'll love this ring you have for me, but I think I want you to give me your body."

After picking Menhit up, Aric carried her to the bedroom. "That I can do, but first, I'm going to give you my gift. I promised myself I'd do this right."

Aric put her down so she stood at the foot of the bed. He went over to his dresser and opened the top drawer. Fishing around inside it, he smiled when he pulled his hand out with a blue velvet-covered jewelry box in it. He walked back to Menhit and then went down on one knee while he looked at her lovingly before he opened what he held. A single round-cut diamond set in a simple gold band sat inside.

Aric cleared his throat. "I know the diamond isn't very big, and as a goddess you've probably gotten larger ones, but it was the best I could afford. Anyway, Menhit, will you marry me?"

Menhit gave him a radiant smile and nodded. "Yes, I'll

marry you. And the diamond is more priceless because it is you who gave it to me."

Standing, Aric took the ring out of the jewelry box and placed it on Menhit's ring finger on her left hand. It fit perfectly. "Beautiful. Just like the woman who wears it."

Aric pulled her close and placed his lips on hers. He kissed her with all the love he felt for her. Now that she wore his ring, it seemed more real that they'd be together forever. Once their kiss grew more intense, he picked her up and placed Menhit onto the bed.

He kissed her slowly, deeply as Menhit wrapped her arms around him. Aric cupped her breast and rubbed his thumb back and forth across her taut nipple. Lying between her spread thighs, the head of his cock pressed against her slick opening, he felt as if he'd died and gone to heaven. The woman beneath him stirred his body, bringing him to full arousal with a few strokes of her hand.

Needing the feel of her closing around him, Aric pushed his cock inside Menhit's welcoming heat. With his weight supported on his bent arms, he moved in and out of her. She locked gazes with him. The look of love she gave him had his cock hardening even more.

He set a faster pace when Menhit wrapped her legs around his waist. Their heavy breathing filled the room as he pushed them closer and closer to climax. Once the first wave of her orgasm hit her, Aric groaned loudly as he too reached his. They lay panting, clinging to one another. Forever wouldn't be nearly enough to show her how much he loved her, but he'd gladly spend the rest of eternity trying to.

The End

THE GODDESS' GIRDLE

When Cayden picks up the girdle he finds in the basement of the Royal Ontario Museum, his mind is filled with images of a beautiful woman. She becomes all he can think about, and he's convinced he's losing his sanity — until she appears in his apartment, pushes him to the floor and has wild, hot sex with him.

Shesmetet is an Egyptian goddess who lives in the immortal realm, but as soon as she sees Cayden, she knows he's her mate, the one who will make her complete. For them to be together, Shesmetet will have to learn to live in the mortal realm...and Cayden will have to give up his life as he knows it.

CHAPTER ONE

Cayden Granger looked at the clock that hung on his office wall, pleased to see it was almost lunchtime. He'd arranged to meet his friend, Neil, for lunch. They worked at the ROM, the Royal Ontario Museum, in Toronto. Neil was an Egyptologist, while Cayden worked as a graphic designer.

Cayden walked to the basement. Neil had planned to work all day down there. The museum had received some new Egyptian artifacts the other day, and it was Neil's job to catalogue them and decide which ones would go on display and which would go into storage.

He found Neil working alone at one of the long worktables. Neil looked up as Cayden approached. "Lunchtime already? I thought I just got down here."

Cayden snorted. "It's after twelve. I figured I'd have to get you. Once you're with your artifacts, nothing else seems to exist."

Neil chuckled. "So true. And there are some really great pieces here to keep me distracted from the outside world."

"Like that one?" Cayden asked, nodding to the belt that had a bunch of beads hanging from it.

"Exactly." Neil picked it up, holding it so they hung down. "This is believed to be the Shesmet girdle, which is supposed to be associated with the Egyptian goddess Shesmetet."

"Okay," Cayden said. "Like that means anything to me."

"Ah, come on. You can't tell me you're not just a little bit interested."

Cayden eyed the belt and the beaded apron attached to it. "What's it supposed to do?"

Neil shook his head and rolled his eyes. "It doesn't *do* anything. I guess its only claim to fame is that it was worn by kings during the early dynastic period and the Old Kingdom."

"Like that just didn't go over my head." Cayden made a face as he looked closer at the girdle. "It looks a bit on the feminine side for a man, if you ask me. And, personally, I wouldn't be caught dead wearing that thing."

"A little insecure in your masculinity? I don't know, Cayden, it may be just what you need to attract that lucky lady who'll one day be yours." Neil stood and placed the girdle around Cayden's waist. Neil held it there, then shook his head. "Nope, I thought wrong. The girdle just isn't for you. You couldn't pull it off even if you wanted to."

Cayden stiffened as a jolt of energy shot through him where the girdle touched him. He almost gasped out loud as his mind suddenly filled with the images of a beautiful woman. Her brown eyes seemed to look right through him. Her long, black hair fell around her shoulders and her lush lips parted as she held out her hands. And the dress she wore was some kind of tight, pale yellow linen sheath dress that fell to her shins, hugging her curvy body in all the right places. A surge of need so intense it made him gasp slammed through him, making his cock grow instantly hard.

"Are you okay, Cayden?" Neil asked with concern. "You look a little funny all of a sudden."

As if he suddenly realized he still held the girdle against Cayden, Neil pulled it away and the images of the woman disappeared, leaving Cayden with an intense longing to see more of her. Instead of snatching up the girdle to see if the images would return, he forced himself to move so he stood on the opposite side of the table.

He cleared his throat. "I'm fine. I'm just hungry. Let's get out of here and get some food."

Neil gave him a stare that said he didn't quite believe Cayden. "Okay. Are you sure you aren't coming down with something?"

Cayden ran his gaze over the girdle one last time before he focused back on his friend. "I'm sure. Come on. You need to get out of this basement for a little while. The sun is shining. You do remember what the sun is?"

"Ha, ha. I'm not that bad."

"On a scale of one to ten, I'd say you're about an eight. Now let's haul ass or lunch will be over before we know it."

"I'm coming. You'd swear you hadn't eaten in a week."

Cayden patted his stomach. "You know me. I have a hollow leg."

"It must be all that weightlifting you do. You're all muscle and no—"

"Don't you dare say it, little man, or I'll have to squash you like a bug." At six-foot-four and over two hundred pounds, he dwarfed Neil, who stood at five-eight and had the build of a teenage boy.

"No bug squashing today, please."

As Neil came around the table, Cayden glanced back at the girdle. The urge to pick it up, to touch it, became hard to ignore. He gave himself a mental shake. He had to pull it together. Leaving the basement with Neil at his side, Cayden tried not to think about the Egyptian relic or the woman he'd seen in his mind.

* * * *

For the rest of the day, Cayden couldn't stop thinking about the woman. More than once he thought he'd just go to the basement and touch the girdle again, and it wasn't because he became aroused when he thought of her. No, he only wanted to touch it to see if the woman would appear again inside his mind. Somehow he'd coincidentally conjured the woman up when the girdle had been held against him. When he made a mess of a project he worked on because his thoughts had strayed to her yet again, he knew he only lied to himself. Like a horny teenager with his first nudie magazine, all he could think about was getting another look.

Cayden adjusted an erection in his pants for the umpteenth time. He couldn't go on like this. Getting that obsessive over a woman he'd seen in his mind meant he was losing it. He hadn't been this horny over someone of the opposite sex in years. There he was, turned-on to the point of pain by a woman who didn't even exist, except for in his brain.

By the end of the work day, he couldn't take it anymore. Cayden had to return to the basement and touch the girdle. It was either that or go insane.

Unluckily for him, Neil didn't seem to be around. Cayden cursed. *Now what?* About ready to leave, he spotted the girdle on top the worktable where Neil had been working that morning.

Cayden quickly walked over to it and picked up the girdle. Just as when Neil had held it against him, a jolt of energy shot through his hands. Images of the same woman once again played inside his mind, and from the look she gave him, he swore she saw him as well.

The sound of someone clearing their throat brought

Cayden back to his surroundings. He quickly placed the girdle back onto the table and turned to face Neil. The woman had disappeared now that he was no longer touching it.

He turned and gave Neil a smile. "You're back."

Neil gave him a questioning look. "I thought you said the girdle was too girly for you? And here I find you fondling it."

Cayden crossed his arms over his chest. "For your information, I wasn't fondling it. I just wanted a second look at it."

"Whatever you say. So what's up? I thought you'd have been gone by now."

"I thought I'd check to make sure we're still on for Friday night."

Neil picked up the girdle and placed it in one of the numbered drawers that ran along the wall. "Tomorrow night is fine. Do you want me to bring the beer?" he asked as he turned back to face Cayden.

"Yes."

"Sounds like a plan."

"Good. I'm on my way out now, so I'll see you tomorrow morning."

Cayden forced himself to turn and walk away before he did something stupid like try to find some way to take the girdle home. It was pretty pathetic when the thought of seeing the woman in his mind had become the highlight of his day.

* * * *

Cayden arrived at his downtown apartment with a bag of Chinese take-out he'd picked up on the way home. Once he replaced his dress slacks with a pair of blue jeans and his dress shirt with a black t-shirt, he headed to the kitchen to eat.

He'd just started to eat at the table when a loud purr filled the room. Cayden sat with his fork halfway to his mouth as the purring continued. The sound seemed to be coming from under the table. As something grabbed the material of one of his pant legs and gave it a yank, he slowly put down his fork and then his hands on top the table. He pushed back and bent his head to peer under the tablecloth. What he saw had him up so fast his chair toppled over. When a large cat, a lioness to be exact, came out from under the table, he tried to back up, but he only managed to trip over his piece of furniture. With a thud, he fell onto his backside onto the floor.

Cayden bit back a string of curses as the lioness stepped closer, stuck her nose into the crook of his neck and gave him a good sniff. He froze in place at the feel of her raspy tongue coming out and licking the side of his neck. The lioness' purrs seemed to grow louder as she pressed her nose to his.

"Nice kitty," Cayden said softly. "You don't want to eat me. I don't taste very good."

The lioness pulled back slightly, but she kept her gaze on him. Cayden watched with amazement as the outline of the cat's body blurred and shifted. In a matter of seconds, the lioness was gone and in its place stood the woman he'd seen in his mind when he'd touched the girdle. She knelt on the floor next to him and smiled. He should be trying to get away. Do something other than become increasingly aroused as he stared at her. A normal person would be scared shitless at seeing a shape shifter, but for some stupid reason, he wasn't. His brain was clouded with lust. That being the case, he lost the ability to think and just acted. With a growl of need, he pounced on her and bore her to the floor.

*

Shesmetet hadn't been sure how well this mortal would take to her appearing before him, especially in her lioness form, but his reaction when she shifted to her human one surprised her, to say the least. That he didn't seem afraid of what she was made coming to the mortal realm well worth the risk to be with him.

When he had first come in contact with her girdle, an instant connection had formed between them. And through that Shesmetet knew he wouldn't just be *any* mortal to her. He was her mate. The one who would complete her, make her feel whole and her soul sing. The only reason she hadn't rushed to be with him was the very real danger her presence could put him in. Even though she was no longer worshipped for the protection she offered mortals against demons of slaughter, it did not mean they wouldn't sense her presence in the mortal realm. She was charged with the duty of keeping demon-kind out and eradicating the ones who harmed the mortals. More than one had felt the pain of her sharp teeth and claws. Her coming there could very well draw a demon to her mate, for they had learned to sense her presence in the mortal realm, and they would use anyone close to her to try to bring her down, but the need to be with him had been too much for her to ignore.

As her mate's lips took hers in an open-mouthed kiss, Shesmetet purred and kissed him back. His hands seemed to be everywhere, cupping and stroking her. She felt the length of his erection through his clothing where it pressed against her thigh. She fisted her hands in his longish, dark brown hair and increased the pressure of her mouth. She rocked her hips against his cock, causing wetness to pool between her legs.

This was how she had wanted her mate when she made the decision to come to the mortal realm—fast and hard. No reservations on his part. Being what she was, Shesmetet couldn't stay with him for long. She longed to tell him what he was to her. With a moan of need, she reached between them and cupped his cock through his leg coverings. Her mate seemed to be a big man in every sense of the word.

He lifted his head with a moan and propped himself on his elbows so he could stare down at her. With a shake of his head, he seemed to come back to himself. "What the hell am I doing?"

Shesmetet leaned up and ran her tongue along the inside of his ear. That elicited another moan. "You're about to make love to me." She nipped his chin.

His hazel eyes briefly shut as he pushed his engorged cock against her hand. "I shouldn't."

"Why not?"

"Well, for one thing I have no idea who you are, or what you are. I really don't make it a practice to pounce on beautiful women the instant I see them. Real or imagined. And if I could actually think straight, right about now I'd be freaking out, since you appeared out of nowhere."

Shesmetet chuckled. "I wanted you to pounce." She released his sex, then reached up to caress his cheek. "I am Shesmetet. As for what I am, I'm a goddess, as well as your mate. For now, that is all you need to know. What is my mate's name?" She shoved her hands up his shirt and ran them along his back while she rubbed her hip against his shaft.

"Ahh...ahhh, my name is Cayden. Damn, I can't think straight with you under me like this. You feel too good. I don't understand any of this. And seeing you in that tight dress of yours isn't helping me any."

A smile played along her lips. "All you had to do was ask for me to remove it." Shesmetet willed her dress from her body.

Cayden's eyes dilated with arousal as he gazed at her naked breasts. He drew in a deep breath. "That did *not* help. I can't believe I'm going to say this, but I think we should wait before we have sex. How can you be possible? Where did you come from? And why the hell am I not freaking out? I recognize your name as not just any goddess, but an Egyptian goddess. I must be hanging around Neil too much. His love for everything ancient Egyptian must be rubbing off, and now I'm having hallucinations about an Egyptian goddess. A sexy, gorgeous one that I want take to bed until neither one of us can walk."

Shesmetet couldn't allow Cayden to put off their joining for much longer. With each minute that ticked by, the risk she put him in grew. Only her longing to be with the other half of her soul had pushed her to come to be with him for what little time she had. She didn't have time to try to convince him with words that she was no hallucination.

"No more talking. I need to feel you buried inside me. Now."

Cayden groaned as she pulled his head down and took his lips in a searing kiss. She sucked his tongue inside her mouth, and he seemed to lose his will to resist. His tongue stroked hers while she undid his leg coverings and then shoved her hand inside. She wrapped her hand around his hard length and pumped it up and down. He jerked his hips and moaned. The feel of him, hard and heavy, made her pussy ache to be filled. The empty part of her soul warmed as she touched him. Joining her body to his would drive out the emptiness she felt inside.

After releasing her mouth, Cayden kissed a path along her jaw and down the side of her neck. He pulled her hand away and shifted down her body. With feather-light kisses, he worked his way along her collarbones and down to her breasts. He cupped one in his hand as he swirled his tongue around its taut peak. Shesmetet pressed closer as he did the same to the other before he sucked her nipple into his mouth. He trailed his other hand down between her legs. She moaned when he found her clit and circled it with a finger.

Cayden turned his attention to her other breast. Shesmetet arched her back as he left her clit and moved to the opening of her body. She clutched his shoulders when he pushed a finger and then another inside her core. He pumped his fingers in and out, left her breast and licked a path down to her stomach.

She cried out as he forced her legs farther apart with his shoulders and put his tongue where his fingers had been. "Yes," she moaned. "Just like that."

Shesmetet's orgasm inched closer. Cayden licked and sucked her clit. It felt so good to have him pleasure her with his mouth. She rocked her hips against him, needing more. She whimpered with need. He spread her folds and jabbed his stiffened tongue inside. It was enough to send her over the edge. Threading her fingers in his hair, she moaned, her climax taking her over.

Cayden crawled back up her body. "I can't wait any longer."

He dragged his short-sleeved tunic over his head and then threw it away. He pushed his leg coverings down past his hips, his hard cock bobbing with his movements. Unable to wait for him to remove them the rest of the way, Shesmetet willed them away. She spread her thighs wider when he came to settle between them. The tip of his cock brushed against her pussy as he claimed her lips. She wrapped her legs around his waist after he reared back and then plunged inside.

While he pumped between her legs, Shesmetet squeezed her inner muscles around his shaft. He filled her to capacity. Their two bodies fit perfectly together. As he moved inside her, she gloried in the feel of his hard cock stretching her. His thick length stroked her clit with each thrust. He braced his upper body on his hands and rammed into her harder, faster. His deep moans filled the room while he slid in and out of her pussy.

She clutched his shoulders, another orgasm building. This time when she climaxed, Cayden came with her. As she rode her release, he threw back his head and moaned. He rammed into her one final time, his cock pulsing deep inside her. Out of breath, he collapsed on top her.

Shesmetet wanted nothing more than to lie in her mate's arms for the rest of the night, but it couldn't be. Cupping his face in her hands, she gave him a hard kiss. "I must go."

Cayden kissed the tip of her nose. "I'm not ready for you to run off just yet. The night is far from over. I want you again, but this time in the bed."

She shook her head. "I can't." Oh, how she wished she could. Their bodies still joined, Cayden's cock already started to harden once again.

He flexed his hips and gave her a crooked grin. "I'll make it well worth your while."

Fisting her hands in his hair, Shesmetet kissed Cayden, knowing it would have to tide her over until she felt ready to take the chance to come to him again, if ever. She then did the hardest thing she had ever had to do—she willed herself to the immortal realm.

CHAPTER TWO

C ayden rolled over onto his back and groaned, fully
aware he lay naked on the kitchen floor. He flung
an arm over his eyes. Shesmetet had just
disappeared into thin air. If he still didn't have the taste of
her in his mouth, or her scent on his skin, he could have
almost convinced himself that she hadn't been real. That
he hadn't made love to a goddess, after she'd shape-
shifted from a lioness. Goosebumps spread over his skin
just thinking about it.

Holy crap! He'd just made love to an Egyptian goddess.

Yes, he had, but it wasn't as if he could tell anyone
about it. They'd drag him away in a straightjacket if he so
much as uttered a word of it. The rational, levelheaded
side of him wanted to reason away what had happened.
There really wasn't any way he could not accept Shesmetet
had been as real as he when his body still held traces of
their intimacy.

He slammed the side of his fisted hand on the floor.
Why had she left? She'd disappeared almost as suddenly as
she'd appeared. His mind swam with a million
unanswered questions and his body ached with unfulfilled

desire. The one time hadn't been enough.

Sitting up, Cayden ran his hands through his hair. Now what? He wanted Shesmetet to come back, but he had no idea how to get in contact with her. The only connection he knew of was the girdle, which would be safely locked up in the ROM at this time of night.

Cayden cursed and picked his t-shirt off the floor. Looking around for his jeans, he couldn't find them. He guessed when Shesmetet had made them disappear into thin air before they'd made love his jeans hadn't poofed back after she'd left. He headed to his bedroom to put on another pair before he returned to the kitchen. He righted the chair where it still lay and then sat. The Chinese food was cold, but he couldn't be bothered to heat it up.

While he chewed, he thought over the brief, very brief, conversation that had taken place between him and Shesmetet before they'd made love. She'd told him she was his mate, and he was hers. How she knew that the instant she'd met him, Cayden had no idea. And being mates sounded so permanent. True, he lusted after her, and had the instant he'd seen her inside his mind, but his feelings weren't that deep. He *was* obsessing over her, something he'd never experienced with another woman. Who knew how long that would last. Given his track record, it could be over in a matter of weeks. A small part of him, deep down inside, felt that wouldn't be the case with her. Even now, all he could think about was having her again, being around her, learning more about who and what she was.

Cayden spent the remainder of the evening watching television. Once the hour grew late, he forced himself to go to bed. He still had to get up early for work the next day. Disappointed that Shesmetet hadn't returned, he dragged himself to his room.

* * * *

After a fitful sleep where he'd tossed and turned for most of the night, Cayden woke up feeling like crap. It didn't help any that he also woke up with a raging hard-on. He blamed that on the erotic dreams he'd had of Shesmetet.

Cranky and out of sorts, Cayden got out of bed and then headed for the shower. It helped clear the cobwebs out of his head, but it did nothing for the erection he still sported. He'd thought of relieving himself, but it wouldn't last long. All it'd take to get him aroused again would be thoughts of Shesmetet. If the morning turned out to be any indication of what his day would be like, Cayden had a feeling it wouldn't be pleasant. As far as he could tell, the only bright spot of the day would be when he could touch the girdle—at least, he hoped it would be. He decided to pick Neil's brain about Shesmetet. Cayden wanted to know everything about her.

He left early for lunch and headed down to the basement of the museum. He figured Neil would still be working down there. Sure enough, Cayden found Neil bent over another artifact at the same table where he'd worked yesterday. He looked down the length of the table where his friend worked and noticed the girdle wasn't with the other pieces spread out on it. Damn. Now he had to somehow bring it up in conversation.

When Neil didn't look up, Cayden loudly cleared his throat. "Are you ready for lunch?"

Neil glanced up at him, then at his watch. "Aren't you a bit early?"

Cayden cleared his throat again and tried to sound nonchalant. "No girdle today?"

"No. Not today."

"I want to see it," he blurted. *Real smooth, Cayden*, he thought. "I mean, can I see it again?"

Neil gave him an odd look before he said slowly, "It's

in drawer number nineteen."

Cayden walked to the shallow drawer and then pulled it open. The girdle lay on the bottom. His heart beat faster as he reached inside and gently touched it with a finger. Zilch. Nada. Nothing happened when he brushed against one of the beads. No images of Shesmetet appeared inside his mind. No jolt of energy. With his back to Neil, he closed his eyes for a few seconds and took a deep breath. A sense of disappointment swept through him, as well as an intense wave of longing for Shesmetet.

He slowly closed the drawer, and said, "You told me yesterday that the girdle was probably associated with the Egyptian goddess Shesmetet. What do you know about her?" He turned around to find Neil staring at him as if he'd suddenly grown two heads.

"Why the sudden interest in the girdle and a goddess?"

Cayden walked to Neil. "I'm just interested, all right? Maybe you're starting to rub off on me, Mr. Egyptologist. Are you going tell me or not?"

"No need to get touchy. I don't know a whole lot about Shesmetet, but I'll tell you what I do. She is a protective goddess. She was called on to protect against demons of slaughter."

Given the size of Shesmetet, Cayden had a hard time believing she could protect anyone from a demon. The top of her head would barely reach his shoulder. "How exactly did she do that?"

"Supposedly with magical spells. Sorry, but that's all I know."

Cayden nodded. "Okay. That's more than I knew before." He pulled out a chair on the other side of the table and sat. "I guess I'll wait here until you're ready to go."

Neil stared at him. "Are you sure you're all right, Cayden? You aren't exactly acting like yourself right now. Maybe it isn't such a great idea for me to come over tonight."

Sitting alone for another night in his apartment while he pined for Shesmetet was the last thing Cayden wanted. If anything, a few beers with Neil should help keep his mind off her for a little while.

"I'm fine. You're not canceling on me tonight. We both need to kick back with a few beers and enjoy a movie. You work too hard."

"Are you sure?" Neil asked.

"Of course I'm sure. Now shut up and get back to work so we can get something to eat sometime soon."

Neil chuckled. "I just need a few more minutes."

Cayden silently watched Neil. Thoughts of Shesmetet and how it'd felt to hold her flitted through his mind. He wanted her back, but since he hadn't been able to "see" her when he'd touched the girdle, he had a feeling he wouldn't be seeing her again any time soon. Surprisingly, that thought hurt more than he would have expected.

* * * *

After a long day of work, Cayden went home to his empty apartment. Even though she wouldn't be there, the first thing he did when he walked through the door was look for Shesmetet. He shouldn't have felt disappointed when he didn't find her, but that didn't stop him from feeling it, anyway. Most of the time at work he'd thought of her, unable to get her out of his mind. He was well and truly obsessed. If she'd been a mortal woman and she hadn't wanted to have anything to do with him, he could picture himself turning into a stalker. Not a good thought.

Once he changed out of his work clothes, Cayden whipped up a quick meal, which he ate in the living room. He didn't know if he'd ever again be able to go into his kitchen and not think of how he'd made love to Shesmetet on the floor.

An hour later, and right on time as usual, Neil rang his

buzzer to be let up to the apartment. Cayden met him at the door before he ushered him inside. "I'll take that," he said as he took the six-pack of beer. Cayden opened the carton and then handed a beer to his friend. "Here, take this and sit in the living room. I'll just stick the rest in the fridge."

That done, Cayden opened a beer for himself and then went to join Neil in the living room. He turned on the DVD player before he stuck in the movie he'd rented. "This is supposed to be good."

"As long as it has a few good explosion scenes and fast-paced action, it's all good."

Cayden chuckled. "Then this should be right up your alley." For a man who'd chosen a career of digging up moldering bones and studying musty relics, Neil liked his movies full of shootouts, car chases and things that blew up.

Halfway through the movie, Cayden thought he heard a sound coming from his bedroom. He cocked his head in that direction and waited, but it didn't come again. A few minutes later, it came again, this time louder. It sounded as if someone walked around inside his room.

Deciding to investigate, Cayden got up. Neil, who'd become totally engrossed in the movie, didn't say anything when Cayden walked out of the living room. Inside his bedroom, he turned on the light. He grunted in surprise as he found himself slammed up against the wall as Shesmetet threw herself into his arms. She tunneled her fingers through his hair and brought his head down to devour his mouth. Cayden wrapped his arms around her waist and hauled her against him while he kissed her back. He was about to walk her backward toward his bed when he heard the sound of a loud explosion coming from the television.

Cayden disentangled Shesmetet's hands from his hair and put some space between them. "You came back," he said quietly.

"I couldn't stay away any longer. I'm just not strong enough. I need to be with you. I don't want to give you up."

When Shesmetet would have stepped back into his arms, Cayden put some more distance between them. "Wait. I have company over."

Shesmetet gave him a coy look as she reached out and stroked his chest before she cupped the bulge in the front of his jeans. "Then make him leave. I want you in your bed, naked, with my mouth all over you."

Cayden groaned and his cock hardened beneath her palm. He took hold of her wrist and pulled her hand away. "I'll get rid of Neil, but this time we aren't going to have drive-by sex. Understand? We're going to talk first, then we'll have our fun."

Shesmetet opened her mouth to say something, but Cayden silenced her with his lips. He gave her a hard kiss before he pulled away and left the bedroom, making sure he shut the door behind him. Cayden hurried into the living room and hit the stop button on the DVD player.

"Hey," Neil protested. "The movie isn't over yet. And it was at a good part too."

Once he had the DVD out of the player, Cayden put it in its case and gave it to Neil. "Here, take it home with you so you can watch the end. Sorry, but I have to cut the evening short." He hurried Neil to the apartment door.

Neil stared at him. "Is something wrong? Are you feeling okay?" He looked at Cayden closer. "Your hair is sticking up on end in places and you look a little flushed."

Cayden quickly ran his fingers through his hair. "Yeah, that's it. I think I've come down with something. My stomach feels kind of funny."

"I'm out of here then. I don't need to get whatever you have. Are you sure you don't mind if I take the movie home?"

"No." Cayden opened the apartment door and gestured for Neil to leave.

"All right then. I'll bring it to work with me on Monday."

"Sounds good."

Cayden shut and then locked the door as soon as Neil stepped out into the hallway. Neil now taken care of, Cayden rushed back to his bedroom. Shesmetet lay naked on his bed with the sheets only up to her waist.

He shook his head. "Oh no, you don't. I told you we were going to talk first."

Shesmetet flipped back the covers to reveal the rest of her. She patted the space next to her on the mattress. "Take your clothes off and come lie next to me. We don't have much time."

Cayden crossed his arms over his chest, mostly to stop himself from doing what she'd asked. "No. I won't take my clothes off until we've had a little chat." No sooner had he said those words his clothes disappeared, leaving him completely naked. "Now you're just not playing fair." His cock become fully engorged as Shesmetet lowered her gaze to it and licked her lips. The woman would be the death of him yet. "I'm not getting into that bed until you at least tell me what the hurry is all about."

Shesmetet's face grew serious as she moved her gaze up to his face. "It's not safe."

"What isn't safe?"

"Me being here with you in the mortal realm."

"Why?"

"Because they could follow me to you."

"Who are they?" Cayden felt as if he were pulling teeth just to get the answers he wanted out of Shesmetet.

With a heavy sigh, she sat up and pulled the covers over her chest. "Demons. They can sense my presence when I'm in the mortal realm. Since I'm one of their greatest foes, they will track me down and try to do me harm. The shorter time I spend here the harder it is for them to pinpoint where I am exactly. I shouldn't be here. I put you at risk, but I can't stay away from you."

Cayden went and sat on the bed next to Shesmetet. "So, you want to have a quickie then disappear again? What if I don't want that? What if I want you to stay the night instead?"

"I told you why I can't stay."

"That's not a good enough reason, Shesmetet. I'm a big boy. I can look after myself, and who's to say any demons will come."

Shesmetet gave him a wry look. "They'll come. They always do."

"They haven't yet."

"It's only a matter of time."

Cayden sighed. "There's a connection between us, but that doesn't mean I'm going to sleep with you only to lose you the second we complete the act. I'll start to feel a little used, especially since I have no way to get in contact with you. Now I don't even have the girdle as a go-between since it didn't seem to work today."

"I severed our connection with it to keep you safe."

Cayden sighed. "I know you feel you're looking out for my welfare, but at least let me have a say in your decisions since they affect me as well." He picked up one of her hands and laced their fingers together. "Stay the night with me." When she didn't say anything, he asked, "What will your answer be, Shesmetet? Will you stay the night? If your answer is no, I want you to leave. So which will it be?"

CHAPTER THREE

Cayden forced himself not to say anything else while he waited for Shesmetet to answer. He could practically see the wheels turning in her head as she thought it over. He really didn't want her to leave, but being used by a woman just to scratch an itch didn't appeal to him, no matter how badly he wanted her. And he wanted her—bad.

Shesmetet gave him a sad smile. "I just found you. I don't want to give you up."

"Then don't. You're a goddess. You must be powerful enough to do some damage to a demon. You may think staying away will protect me, but who's to say they don't already know about your visits here and aren't waiting to catch me alone to draw you out?" Her eyes widened. Cayden gave her a half smile. "There, you see? You can keep me much safer if you stay." He leaned in and kissed the corner of her mouth. "It'll give us a lot more time to enjoy each other."

With a breathy sigh, Shesmetet turned her head, letting Cayden kiss the side of her neck. "Mmm. You win. I'll stay."

"That's all I needed to hear."

Cayden gathered her close and took her mouth in a hard kiss. He pushed his tongue past her lips as he lowered her onto the bed. Shesmetet wrapped her arms around his neck. He pulled the sheet that covered her out from between them. He moaned at the feel of her taut nipples brushing against his chest. Now that he had her under him, he wanted to touch and taste every inch of her, but she had other ideas.

With a shove, she pushed him onto his back. She straddled his thighs as she left his mouth and trailed kisses along his jaw to his ear. She swirled her tongue inside it, making him shiver. She nipped his earlobe. His heart beat faster as she shifted lower and placed her lips across his chest and down to his nipple. Shesmetet dragged her teeth along the small nub before she swirled her tongue around it. Cayden fisted his hand in the sheets beneath him while she continued down to his abs. As she went lower, her long hair tickled his stomach.

"I love the feel of your mouth on me," Cayden moaned.

"I'm going to taste every inch of you," Shesmetet replied in a husky voice.

He jerked his hips when her warm breath hit the tip of his cock. She trailed her fingers down his shaft, then back up to the head, drawing a long moan out of him. The first brush of her tongue as she circled the head of his shaft made Cayden lift his head to watch her pleasure him. The sight of her laving the length of him made him harden even more.

Shesmetet's purrs filled the room as she took a firm hold of his erection and slipped him inside her mouth. The feel of her sucking on his cock as she slid it in and out almost made Cayden come right then. With a groan, he fought it back. When he did come, he wanted to be buried to the hilt inside her pussy, hearing her moan his name with her own release. Her mouth on him as she squeezed the base of his shaft had him lifting his hips off the mattress in time with her strokes. She took more of his length and purred again. The sound vibrated along his shaft, shooting waves of pleasure down the length of him to his balls.

Knowing he couldn't take much more, Cayden tugged on her arm. "Enough. Put me inside you."

She swiped her tongue along the length of his shaft one final time before she crawled up his body. With her hands braced on either side of his head, she positioned herself over him. She pushed down until she'd completely impaled herself on his thick shaft.

Cayden grasped Shesmetet's hips as she slowly rode him up and down. Being deep inside her, with her inner walls squeezing around his shaft, he wouldn't last very long. He lifted his head off the pillow and sucked the nipple that hovered so invitingly in front of him into his mouth. She moaned as he alternated between drawing on her nipple and swirling his tongue around the taut peak. She rode him faster, harder, causing him to lift his hips to match the pace she set. His cock grew even harder, and she whimpered with pleasure.

Knowing he'd soon reach the point of no return, Cayden released her nipple and placed a finger where their bodies were joined. "Come for me, Shesmetet."

He looked down as he stroked Shesmetet's clit. The sight of his cock sliding in and out of her wet pussy pushed his arousal even higher. Unable to look away, he continued to pound into her until he pushed her over the edge into a climax. Her head fell back with a moan while her inner walls spasmed around him, fisting his cock. Cayden's climax tore through him as he grabbed her hips to hold her to him. Wave after wave of pleasure shot through him.

Shesmetet collapsed onto his chest. Cayden held her tight while they fought to catch their breath. As she lay with her head nestled under his chin, he realized sex with her didn't even compare to what he'd experienced in the past.

Shesmetet lifted her head. He couldn't help but notice how her lips were puffy from his kisses. "Do you need to sleep?"

Cayden chuckled. "Not yet. Why do you ask?"

She took her lower lip between her teeth while she stroked his chest. "I want to make love again, but I know mortals need much more sleep than the gods. I don't want to tire you out."

He shook his head and snorted. "I'm by no means tired. I intend to put this night to good use."

Shesmetet moved off him and snuggled up against his side with her head pillowed on his chest. "That's good."

Cayden sucked in a breath as she reached down and trailed her fingers along his shaft. Surprisingly, his cock stirred. Even though they'd just made love, he still hungered for her. He didn't think he'd ever get enough. She took his cock in her hand and pumped it up and down. He sucked in a sharp breath. He let her pleasure him that way until he was once again fully erect.

After pulling her hand away, he shifted so he lay on his side, facing her. He claimed her lips in a kiss as he stroked down her waist to her thigh. Cupping her bottom, he urged her closer, then hooked her leg over his arm. Cayden lifted it, opening her just enough for him to rub his hard cock against her sex without entering her.

He continued to tease her in this way until his shaft became coated with her wetness. He watched Shesmetet's face while he slowly pushed the tip of his cock inside her pussy. She was beautiful. While she gasped and moaned with pleasure, he pushed another inch of his shaft inside her core.

"Why can't I get enough of you, Shesmetet?"

She reached up and cupped his cheek. "Because we

were meant to be together."

A rush of feelings washed over him. He wanted to proclaim to the world that this woman was his and that he never wanted to let her go. The thought of her leaving him made his chest ache. A part of him would be missing if she ever left him and didn't return. Somehow, in such a short period of time, Shesmetet had wormed her way inside him.

Holding her tighter, Cayden asked softly, "It's as if I'm addicted to you. I can't get enough of your taste, your touch. I feel as if you've always been with me. It's never been like this for me before."

Shesmetet cupped his cheek. "It's the same for me, Cayden. It's the way of mates."

They both moaned when he gave her another inch of his cock. "Is this lust or is it love? It feels a lot stronger than ordinary lust, but how can this be love? We hardly know each other. You can't fall in love with someone you just met."

She placed her hand on his chest over his heart. "What is your heart telling you, Cayden? It knows. It recognized me as your mate when you first saw me in your mind when you touched my girdle, just as my heart recognized you. We're supposed to fall in love at first sight. If not, the connection would never have been made."

Knowing exactly what Shesmetet meant to him, Cayden pulled back, then entered her completely with one thrust. She held on to his shoulder as he pounded into her. He had wanted to take her slowly, but the need to possess her, claim her as his, overrode that. He realized he'd been searching for her for most of his adult life. With her in his arms, he felt as if he could take on the world and win. He felt complete, whole. She humbled him. Her whimpers of need urged him to go faster, harder. He rammed into her over and over again until they cried out, coming together.

Cayden lowered her leg and gently brushed a kiss

across her mouth. After pulling the sheet over them, he wrapped an arm around Shesmetet's waist and tucked her head under his chin. His eyes fluttered shut. He'd take a little nap, then he'd show his mate how much he needed her again and again.

* * * *

As the first light of dawn broke over the horizon, Shesmetet quietly slipped out of bed. She smiled down at Cayden, who still slept on. Her mate had turned out to be an insatiable lover.

Turning away, Shesmetet softly tiptoed out of the room, still naked. She decided to use the time while Cayden slept to bathe. Not really sure where to find his bathing room, she closed the bedchamber door behind her and then walked down the hall to the only other door that stood open. She poked her head inside and smiled when she spotted the large white tub.

The only light came from the single curtained window at the end of the bathing chamber. Not really bothered, since she could see just as well in dim light as in bright, she stepped inside and walked to the tub. She frowned when she looked at the spout positioned over it and the single knob on the tiled wall above it. Shesmetet took hold of the knob and turned. Nothing happened. She turned it the other way. Still nothing happened.

Not wanting to have to wake Cayden for help, Shesmetet scowled at the knob. She was a goddess. She could figure this out. With a firmer hold, she turned it hard. This time it pulled out slightly. A trickle of water dripped from the spout and into the tub. She pulled harder and was rewarded with a gush of water. Now that she had it turned on she had to still figure out how to keep the water from draining away and to make it warmer. It didn't take her long to accomplish both those things.

While the tub filled, Shesmetet stepped inside and sat. The warm water lapped around her as the level rose. The mortal realm had changed so much. The mortals had found ways to make their lives easier since she'd last visited. She realized she had a lot to learn about her mate's world, especially if she wanted to fit into it. A small smile played across her lips. She'd never thought of spending much time in the mortal realm until now. She came when she had been summoned to defeat demons, only to return to the immortal realm once her task was complete.

When her thoughts shifted to demons, she stiffened. All during the night while Cayden had made love to her, she had not once thought about them. She'd now been in the mortal realm for hours. The demons should already have been aware of her presence, but so far, they had left her alone, which was something they had never done in the past. They usually would try to use this opportunity to destroy her, to rid themselves of her permanently.

Shesmetet turned off the water now that the tub had filled and leaned back. Maybe the demons no longer had any interest in mortals, though she found that hard to believe. The demons lived to torture and kill mortals for the sport of it.

She closed her eyes and relaxed in the warm bath water. Her eyes snapped open a minute later at the sound of Cayden bellowing her name. "Cayden," she called back. "I'm in here."

Cayden rushed into the bathing chamber and then scooped her out of the tub before he held her tight. "When I woke up and you weren't in bed, I thought you'd left again," he said as he kissed her forehead.

Shesmetet stroked his back. "I told you I would stay. I just thought to bathe while you slept."

He put her down on her feet, but didn't let her go. "Why didn't you wake me up? I could have helped you."

"You were tired and needed to sleep." There were dark

circles under Cayden's eyes. "And from the look of you, you need to go back to sleep."

"Don't you? You couldn't have slept long."

"I had all the sleep I needed. A couple hours are all my body requires each night. Go back to bed, Cayden. I'll return to the bedchamber once I finish my bath."

Cayden shifted her in his arms, cupped her bottom and brought her up against his half-aroused cock. "Why don't I just join you in the bathtub?"

She shook her head, got him to put her down and stepped back into the tub. "Not now. Another time you can join me in my bath. Right now, I want you to sleep. You need that more."

He covered his mouth with his hand and yawned. "You're killing me. Fine, but once I'm caught up on my sleep, I want you back in my arms. I like you there."

She was tempted to change her mind, but she held firm to her decision. With her finger pointed to the open door, she said, "Out

"I'm going, I'm going." Before he left the bathing room, he handed her a bar of soap that sat near the sink and then put a towel that he took off a shelf above the counter on it. "Just don't take too long or I'll come back to get you." Cayden walked out.

Using the soap, Shesmetet pondered what Cayden had said about her killing him. He hadn't meant it literally, but nonetheless, it made her think of his mortality. She would have to change that soon. If they were to be true mates, she wanted an eternity with him. That meant she would have to turn him into an immortal.

Feeling as if her life was now complete with Cayden in it, Shesmetet hurried to finish her bath. Once he woke up again, they would have a lot to talk about, first being the eternity they would have together.

CHAPTER FOUR

The sound of birds chirping loudly outside his bedroom window brought Cayden awake. Even before he had his eyes fully open, he reached for Shesmetet. He smiled when he saw she lay on her side next to him.

"Good morning." He placed a light kiss on her lips.

"Good morning. Did you sleep well?"

Cayden pushed her onto her back and settled between her legs. "Yes. Would you like to continue where we left off in the bathroom?" Before Shesmetet could answer, his stomach growled loudly. He cringed. "Now that was real romantic."

Shesmetet giggled. "Maybe we should wait until after you have eaten."

His stomach protested its emptiness once again. "I guess food is in order. You must be hungry as well." As Shesmetet gave him a sheepish look, Cayden shook his head. "Let me guess, you don't need to eat," he said.

"I'm a goddess, Cayden. I'm not mortal like you."

Cayden grew serious. "Shesmetet, how *is* this going to work between us? As you said, you're an immortal

Egyptian goddess and I'm just a mortal. You'll live forever while I'll grow old and eventually die."

When he would have said something more, Shesmetet placed a finger against his lips. "It doesn't have to be that way," she said softly.

He pulled her finger away. "I don't understand."

"You are my mate, Cayden. If you wish it, I can give you immortality. You wouldn't be a god, but you would still live forever, with me."

Cayden wanted to tell her yes, that he wanted to be with her for an eternity, but he thought of his family. He was his parents' only child and he had a close relationship with them. If he became immortal, they'd eventually notice he'd stopped aging.

He brushed a lock of hair off her forehead. "If I say yes, what about my family? Would I have to keep this a secret?" he asked.

Shesmetet looked at him solemnly. "As a general rule, it is forbidden for mortals to know that we as gods can grant them immortality."

"These are my parents I'm talking about here, Shesmetet. They only had me. I don't have any brothers or sisters to take my place if I up and disappear."

"It wouldn't have to be right away, Cayden."

"I would have to move away, quit my job and start off fresh somewhere else? Move to wherever you live when you aren't here in the mortal realm?"

She shook her head. "You can't ever live in the immortal realm. It would be forbidden even if you were an immortal. Only the gods can live there."

Cayden sighed and rolled over onto his back next to Shesmetet. "There seems to be a lot of rules when it comes to mortals. To me, it looks as if the gods get to do whatever the hell they want with no rules to follow."

Shesmetet rolled onto her side and propped herself on her elbow so she could look down at him. "It's not like that. We have rules we must follow as well. If we break them, then we must answer to Ra."

"Okay, then what is one of these rules you can't break?"

"The only time a god can give a mortal immortality is if that mortal is their mate. And even then the god must have the mortal's permission. We can't force immortality on our mates if they don't wish it."

Cayden locked gazes with Shesmetet. "So you're telling me that if I said that I didn't want to become an immortal you wouldn't do it, even if it meant you'd have to watch me grow old and eventually die?"

"Correct. I may be a goddess, but that doesn't mean I have the right to force my will on you."

"Do I have time to think about this? If my parents didn't factor into my decision, I'd give you a resounding yes right now."

"Of course," she said.

Cayden's stomach growled loudly, reminding him of something else he wanted to ask Shesmetet. "You don't eat. Once I'm immortal, will I no longer need to eat as well?"

She chuckled. "No, you'll still need to eat and drink as you do now."

"Well, that's good news. I enjoy my food too much." He flipped back the covers and sat up. "I guess I'd better get some food into me before my stomach starts eating itself. I'll hop into a quick shower first."

Cayden gave Shesmetet a quick, hard kiss before he slipped out of bed. He wanted nothing more than to stay there and make love to her all day, but his empty stomach would no longer be ignored. She'd given him a lot to think about. Being offered immortality was something he never would have dreamed would happen to him. Before meeting her, he would have laughed off the very idea. Only crazy or delusional people believed in stuff like a goddess offering a mortal the chance to live for eternity.

After sweeping her delectable body with his gaze one last time, he sighed wistfully as he forced himself to turn around and walk away.

* * * *

Once Cayden had showered and then gotten something to eat, he joined Shesmetet, who stood in front of his living room window, looking outside. She'd put on the same dress she'd worn the night before. Since she stood with her back to him, he ran his gaze down to her bottom. The dress hugged it to perfection.

Pulling his gaze off her ass, he went to stand next to Shesmetet. Her expression of longing as she stared at the city street below told Cayden she wouldn't want to stay cooped up in his apartment all day.

He put his arm around her shoulders and kissed the top of her head. "How about we get out of the apartment for a while?"

Shesmetet turned to look at him. "You want to take me outside?"

He smiled. "I know you want to, and I know just the place to go. How would you like to go see the place where I work? The ROM—it's a museum—has a large collection of Egyptian artifacts. There are other things there as well that you might find interesting."

She gave him a smile so bright it almost rivaled the sun. "I would love to go to this ROM. Even though it may overwhelm me a bit—this world of yours is so much larger than it was the last time I came to the mortal realm—I want to learn to fit in. Can we leave now?"

Cayden chuckled at her enthusiasm. "Sure, but you'll have to change your clothes first. Not that you don't look good in that dress," he said as he hungrily skimmed his gaze over her body.

"What is wrong with it?" Shesmetet asked while she

looked down at herself.

"It really isn't the type of dress one would wear when going to a museum."

"Oh. What should I wear then?"

"Uh, maybe something similar to what I have on. Jeans and a t-shirt." Cayden remembered the stack of flyers he'd left on the floor by the apartment door the day before. He went over and picked up the pile of papers and then returned to Shesmetet. He sorted through the flyers until he found one that advertised clothing. "Here," he said as he pointed to a female model who wore a pair of jeans and a pink t-shirt. "Something like this."

Shesmetet stared at the picture, then in a blink of an eye she wore the exact same outfit the woman in the flyer had on, right down to the athletic shoes. "How is this?"

Cayden nodded. "Good, except I forgot to show you what women wear under their t-shirts." He could clearly see the outline of her nipples through the material of her shirt. He quickly flipped through the flyer until he found the section for bras and panties. Cayden pointed to the bra and panty set a model wore. "Women wear these under their clothes. The bra supports your breasts."

"And the other undergarment? Why do they wear that? I noticed you don't wear any under your jeans."

"I prefer to go commando. The only time I wear underwear is when I have to dress for work."

"So you would prefer that I wear those undergarments like mortal women do?"

"Yes." He leaned in and kissed her lips softly. "Later I'll show you how much of a turn-on it is for a man to get a woman undressed down to her bra and panties."

Shesmetet took the flyer and turned her back to him. "In that case, no looking." Once she turned back around, Cayden saw the outline of a bra through her t-shirt. He reached for the flyer to see if he could guess which one she wore, but she held it out of reach. "Oh, no you don't." The flyer disappeared.

"You do realize I won't be able to think of anything else but what you have on under your clothes."

"Then it should make the surprise even better."

Cayden had to give her that. The anticipation would make him enjoy getting her out of her clothes even more, if the wait didn't kill him first. "Let's go. The sooner we leave the sooner I can get you back here so I can undress you."

* * * *

The drive to the ROM proved eventful. Shesmetet had looked at his car with doubt when he'd helped her into the passenger seat. Once he started the car and then pulled out onto the street, her eyes had widened while she painfully clutched his thigh with one hand and pressed her other against the door. Cayden tried to distract her by pointing out landmarks, but that only caused her to dig her nails even harder into his leg.

Thankful that he didn't live too far from the museum, Cayden pulled his car into the parking lot before finding an empty space to park. Once he turned the engine off, he'd had to pry Shesmetet's hand from his thigh so he could get out. When he opened her door, she jumped out so fast she rammed into him. Given her reaction, he had to wonder how he'd get her back into it for the trip home.

As they walked hand in hand toward the front entrance to the ROM, Shesmetet slowly started to relax. "Are you okay now?" Cayden asked.

She nodded. "I'm not sure I like to travel that way," she replied.

"I guess I better not take you out on the highway where cars drive even faster. We'll have to work on getting you used to the car at slower speeds first."

She turned and gave him a look of incredulity. "It goes

faster?"

Cayden bit back a smile. "Yes, a lot faster than I drove here."

Shesmetet paled slightly. "I don't think I'll ever be able to do that."

Deciding he'd better change the subject before she became too scared to ever set foot inside a car again, Cayden held the door open for her to go inside the museum ahead of him, and said, "Let's see the Egyptian collection first, since you should be an expert on it."

Cayden took her hand once again as he led her to the section of the museum that housed the ancient Egyptian artifacts on display. Shesmetet perked up when the first pieces came into view. She flitted from one to the next, sometimes reading out loud the hieroglyphs carved on pieces of stone in Egyptian. He decided he loved the sexy sound of her voice when she spoke her native language just as much as in her accented English. Seeing her like this, enjoying their outing, he found there was a lot about her that he loved. The way she moved, the way she almost glided from one display case to another, the way her long, black hair shined in the overhead lights. He also enjoyed just being with her. Watching her almost glow with enthusiasm with each new relic she saw, his heart melted a little bit more. He couldn't picture his life without her.

Cayden had looked at the Egyptian collection many times with Neil, but with Shesmetet, he saw it in a whole new light. The artifacts were a part of her past life and she had a connection to them. It also brought home how special she really was.

He well and truly loved her. If someone were to have told him a year ago he'd meet and fall in love with a goddess, he would have been the first person to take them to get their head examined by a shrink. Cayden was still wavering on becoming an immortal and having to give up his family. If given time, he could probably come to grips with it.

Then there was the whole demon thing. Even though Shesmetet hadn't brought the subject up again, she still worried for his safety. Having had no dealings with demons before, he had no idea what they were capable of. He just hoped they continued to keep away from Shesmetet.

Once they'd seen every piece in the Egyptian collection, Cayden led Shesmetet to the others. The need to hold her, possess her, built inside him. Each sway of her hips as she walked made him ache to bury his cock inside her. He wanted to make love to her until they could no longer move. Wanting her, he hurried her through one collection to the next. She didn't seem to mind. If anything, she seemed just as eager as he to leave the museum. More than once he caught her glancing down at the crotch of his pants and licking her lips. Each time she'd done it his cock had jerked, which made him ache even more.

After rushing her past the last display cases, Cayden ushered Shesmetet out the museum's doors. With her hand in his, he had them both at his car in less than a minute. She hesitated briefly when he opened the door, but he soon fixed that. He pulled her close and kissed her with all the pent-up desire he felt. After he pulled away, they were breathless.

"The car will make the trip to my apartment go a lot quicker, Shesmetet."

She ran her hand down the front of his body before she stroked the bulge in his pants. She then got into the car. Cayden walked around the back of it and then climbed into the driver's side. This time the drive didn't seem to bother Shesmetet, mostly because she spent the time fondling his cock through his pants up until they reached his apartment building. By some miracle, he managed to park his car without smashing into anything.

Cayden helped Shesmetet out and then led her to the

elevator. By now he sported a noticeable hard-on. As he put the key in the lock to his apartment door, she moved from his side and came to stand between him and the door. She wrapped her arms around his waist and rubbed against him. He had to bite the inside of his cheek to stop the loud moan that threatened to break free.

The door finally unlocked. He opened it and walked Shesmetet backward into the apartment. He slammed it behind them and then locked it. His keys hit the floor as he reached to pull her closer. Cayden took her mouth in a demanding kiss as he ground his erection against her hip. She sucked his tongue into her mouth while she stuck her hands under his t-shirt and caressed his back.

He pushed her against the wall and ran his hands down her sides. Taking hold of the bottom of her t-shirt, he inched it up. He released her mouth so he could pull it all the way off. Cayden stared down at the sheer white lace bra she wore. With a groan, he bent down and stroked his tongue over each lace-covered nipple until they tightened into buds.

Shesmetet yanked his shirt off before she reached to undo the button of his jeans, but Cayden stopped her. If she touched him now, he'd either come in his pants or yank down hers and sink into her. He wanted to take the time to see the panties she wore, to see if they matched her bra. To keep her from touching him, he turned her so she faced away from him. She put her hands on the wall in front of her as he reached around and undid the button and zipper of her jeans.

He dragged his tongue along the back of her neck, and taking hold of the waistband of her pants, he gently eased them down past her hips. Once they fell to pool at Shesmetet's feet, she kicked them free. Cayden ran his hands down her sides to her bottom. He moaned as he encountered bare skin where the back of her panties should have been. Looking down, he moaned again. She wore a white lace thong, the back nothing more than a piece of string. He hadn't known the flyer he'd shown her had thongs in it, but he was glad it had.

Holding her by the hips, Cayden kissed a path down her back to the top of her thong. He went on his knees and nipped the twin globes of her ass. Shesmetet moaned as and licked where he'd bitten. He pulled her hips away from the wall and positioned her so she was partially bent over with her hands still supporting her. He spread her legs with his hands and ran them up the insides of her thighs. At the apex, he yanked her thong aside and ran his tongue along her pussy. She bucked her hips as he stiffened his tongue and pushed it inside her core.

He licked and sucked her pussy while he reached down and undid his jeans. When he shoved them down past his hips, Shesmetet whimpered. Rising behind her, Cayden took hold of her hips and entered her with one hard thrust. He groaned at the sensation of her wet pussy clamping around his aching cock. He pulled back and surged inside again. His cock hardened even more, and she squeezed her inner walls around his shaft. In and out he pumped. She pushed back while he surged inside her. As his orgasm built, he reached around to cup her breast through her bra and tugged her nipple. Once her pussy spasmed around his cock, he pushed into her one final time and exploded deep inside her. Groaning, he held her to him until the last wave of pleasure receded.

Out of breath, Cayden bent and dragged his tongue up her spine. He cried out when a sharp pain radiating from his back washed through him.

Half-sensing someone standing behind him, he turned his head and found a man who stood at his left shoulder, his eyes glowing red. He gave Cayden an evil grin as he yanked out a lethal-looking dagger that he'd shoved between Cayden's shoulder blades. Cayden grunted with pain, and a warm gush of blood dripped down his back.

Suddenly feeling lightheaded, he fell to his knees. The last thing he heard was Shesmetet's cry of anguish, then his world went black.

CHAPTER FIVE

Shesmetet willed her clothes back on her body as she spun around to face the demon who stood behind her. At first glance, he looked human, until she saw his glowing red eyes. He stood as tall as Cayden, and she could easily see his well-muscled body since all he wore was a white Egyptian-style kilt. He curled his upper lip and hissed. The look of hatred he wore was almost a palpable thing between them. She wanted to check Cayden to see how badly he had been wounded, but she had to deal with the demon first. Pushing aside the fear she felt over the amount of blood pooling on the floor around Cayden, she shifted to her lioness form and launched herself at the demon. Her roars filled the apartment as she attacked him with sharp teeth and claws.

She pushed the demon away from Cayden, one of her paws catching him across the chest. "I'll make you pay for that, bitch," he said with a snarl.

In retaliation, the demon slashed out with his dagger. The sharp blade made a deep gash along her ribs, but Shesmetet barely felt it. The sight of Cayden lying in a pool of his own blood had sealed this demon's fate.

Circling each other, the demon taunted her. "Did you think you could stay here undetected? We sensed your presence in the mortal realm when you first came to...visit...your mortal. We figured we would let you have your fun with him, think we wouldn't come, before we took him away from you—permanently. Your claws won't be enough to stop me."

The demon wanted her to shift back to her human form. Only in her lioness one would she be strong enough to defeat him. She let his taunts roll off her back. She would not let him goad her into doing something stupid. Cayden's life was at stake. She couldn't afford to make any mistakes.

She took a swipe at the demon's legs, but he quickly jumped out of reach. "It has been too long since you have fought one of my kind," he said with a sneer. "You are out of practice. I will be no easy kill. And while you try to defeat me, your lover's lifeblood will slowly drain out of him. I can already hear his heart struggling to beat."

With a roar of rage, she launched herself at the demon. While they fought, Shesmetet used her pain and anger to bring the demon down. She tried to sink her teeth into his throat to rip it out, but he brought his fist on top her head, making her briefly see stars. Not to be put off, she sank her claws deeper into him, shredding his skin, weakening him. Once he finally lay battered and bleeding on the floor, she shifted back to human form and used his own dagger to slit his throat. She recited the spell that would send him to the underworld as a message to the other demons so they would know what their fate would be if they too thought to attack her mate.

The battle over, Shesmetet no longer felt the wound in her side as it started to heal. Hurriedly, she went to Cayden. After dropping to her knees, she rolled him to his side. The wound in his back continued to bleed. Seeing the amount of blood already on the floor and the paleness of his face, she knew the demon's blade had to have nicked his heart or a major artery. If she didn't give him immortality now, he would bleed to death in a matter of minutes.

Gently, Shesmetet rolled Cayden over so he lay across her lap while she supported his head in the crook of her arm. Even though he groaned when she moved him, his eyes remained closed. She had to wake him up. He had to consent to what she was about to do.

"Cayden, wake up." His eyes moved back and forth beneath his eyelids, but they didn't open. Shesmetet shook him as she tapped his cheek. "You must wake up." This time they fluttered open.

"Shesmetet?" he asked weakly.

"You have to listen to me closely, Cayden. I must turn you into an immortal or you will die. You have to give me your consent."

Cayden lifted his hand and touched her cheek. "I...I love you." His eyes rolled back up into his head and his hand went limp.

Shesmetet cried out his name while she shook him. "Cayden!"

When he didn't rouse, she placed two fingers at the side of his neck. His pulse was weak. She didn't have much time left. She didn't want to lose him. They were mates, destined to be together forever. She wanted that with Cayden.

With her hand pressed to his pale cheek, Shesmetet gathered her powers and sent a surge of energy through it into Cayden. There should have been a ribbon of energy coming from her, sinking into him, but no connection formed. She shook her head in denial, tears filling her eyes when he remained mortal. This couldn't be happening. Not understanding why her powers failed her now when she needed them the most, she tried again and again to make him immortal.

Every attempt failed.

Wiping the tears from her eyes, she took a deep breath and prepared to do what no god or goddess could do without bringing down the wrath of Ra on them. Shesmetet placed her hand on Cayden's chest over his heart and closed her eyes, focusing deep inside her to her soul. She gathered a small piece of her soul, then sent it along with her powers into him. He gasped as her powers surged through him, permeating every cell in his body. She sent them deeper until they brushed against his soul, and grabbing hold of it, she wrapped the piece of hers around his until they melded into one.

She blinked open her eyes to find Cayden staring at her. He no longer looked pale. She had him sit up so she could run her hand over his wound, which had stopped bleeding and had already started to heal.

Cayden looked at her with a confused expression. "I feel different. The pain is gone, but I don't feel the same."

Shesmetet gave him a watery smile. "I did what needed to be done to save you." She sucked in a breath, feeling herself being pulled to the immortal realm.

His brows drew together. "Shesmetet? What's wrong?"

She tried to fight the pull, but it would be a losing battle. The one who summoned her would not allow her to ignore him for long. She pressed a hard kiss to Cayden's lips. "Whatever happens, always remember I love you."

Cayden reached for her just as she was yanked out of the mortal realm and into the immortal one.

* * * *

She was gone. Cayden had no idea how long he sat on the floor, hoping Shesmetet would return. Minutes then hours went by, but she didn't come back. As darkness fell, he slowly pulled himself together and looked around his apartment. Even though the sun had long set, he found he could see just as well in the dark as he could in the light. His sense of smell had increased too. He now could easily separate individual scents that lingered — the metallic smell of blood, the smell of the food he'd cooked that morning. He breathed deeper as he pulled one out of the many. He savored it, wanting to have it imprinted on him so he'd never forget it — Shesmetet's scent.

Slowly, Cayden pulled himself up onto his feet. He stared down at the large pool of his blood on the floor. The wound he'd received hadn't been a minor one. He realized he was lucky to be alive, considering he should have been dead from that amount of blood loss. He stiffened. There could only be one reason he'd survived — Shesmetet must have given him immortality. It explained why he felt so different. He vaguely remembered her shouting at him to wake up, that she needed his consent. Obviously, she must have taken matters into her own hands, which pleased him since that had been what he wanted. If he'd been able to tell her, he would have quickly given his consent.

Cayden sighed. He had no idea where Shesmetet had gone, but he had a feeling she'd gone back to the immortal realm. Even though he'd been close to death, he'd known Shesmetet had defeated the demon that had attacked them. So it couldn't have been because of the demon the reason she'd left him. He hoped she'd return to him, but he suspected she wouldn't. The thought of her never coming back to him, him having to live for eternity without her at his side, made him ache to have her in his arms again.

With his hands on his hips, he looked at the blood at his feet and then at the other pool of blood in his living room. He needed to clean up the mess. Knowing if Shesmetet had been there she probably would have had the blood gone in a blink of an eye, Cayden waved his hand at the pool at his feet. He had to do a double take when it seemingly disappeared.

He knelt and touched the floor with his fingers. It was if the blood had never been there. "Holy shit. Did I do that?"

Cayden went to the second pool of blood. He looked down at it and waved his hand as he thought of it no longer being there. Sure enough, it disappeared. He slowly backed up until the back of his legs hit the couch, then slumped down on it. *What the hell is going on?*

* * * *

Shesmetet didn't return that night or the next day. Cayden missed her so much he almost physically ached with it. He had no idea why she'd left in the first place, but considering she'd told him she loved him before she'd disappeared, he couldn't help but think she'd been taken against her will. Why and who would have taken her, he had no idea. All he knew is that he wanted her back. It felt as if a piece of him had been ripped out of him, and that he wouldn't feel complete again until he held her in his arms.

He'd also spent the day after her disappearance coming to grips with his new self. Not only could he will things away with a thought, he found he no longer needed to eat or drink. He'd tried to eat something that first night, but had ended up running to the toilet as his body brought it back up again. The same thing had happened when he'd tried to drink water. His sleep patterns had changed as well. After a couple hours of deep sleep, he awoke refreshed as if he'd slept eight or nine. No matter how hard he tried to go back to sleep he couldn't.

All the changes in him also made him think. Shesmetet had told him when she gifted him with immortality that he'd still have the same needs every mortal did only he'd now live forever, which hadn't happened. She'd also said she couldn't give him godhood, but Cayden had to question whether she had. The needs of his body were too similar to hers.

Not ready to face the world, Cayden called in sick on Monday morning. He couldn't tell anyone what had happened. For one thing, they'd think he'd lost it. And if he were to give them the proof that he wasn't crazy, they'd lock him up and experiment on him until they figured out why he could do the things he could. Not something he wanted. He would eventually have to return to work — given long enough, Neil would come knocking to see what was wrong — but Cayden decided he deserved a couple days to sort things out.

With not much else to do, Cayden spent the day watching television. After he grew bored with that, he turned it off and decided to take a shower. While he stood under the running water, he thought of Shesmetet. He had no idea what he'd do if she never returned. Did he want to live forever without her at his side? Not really. The idea of an eternity without her seemed pretty bleak.

As the shower curtain snapped open, Cayden stiffened, prepared to fight off another attack. The sight of Shesmetet in his bathroom with a smile just about sent him reeling. He grabbed her around the waist and pulled her into the shower with him. His lips came down on hers just as the sheath dress she wore disappeared. He threaded his fingers through her hair and slanted his mouth over hers. With a growl of need, he backed her up against the shower's tiled wall. She gripped his shoulders as he raised her leg and put it around his waist.

He lifted his head as he rubbed his cock against her pussy. "I need to be inside you, Shesmetet. Now."

Shesmetet arched against him. "I'm more than ready for you," she said on a moan.

As he pushed his cock inside her pussy he found her wet and ready as she'd said. Cayden took her hard and fast against the wall with the warm water from the shower pounding on them. The sounds of their moans filled the bathroom as they came together.

Cayden let Shesmetet slowly slide down his body to stand on her feet. He cupped her face and gently kissed her lips. "What happened to you? Where did you go?"

"Ra called me before him."

"Why?"

"To answer for what I had done."

Cayden locked gazes with her. "For what you did to me. You didn't just make me an immortal, did you, Shesmetet?"

She shook her head. "I didn't want to lose you. So I did the only thing that would save you. I gave you a piece of my soul as well as immortality. I made you a god, Cayden."

"What did Ra do?"

Shesemetet smiled. "He banished me. I no longer can return to the immortal realm."

Cayden pulled her close. "I'm sorry, Shsemetet. What about the demons? It was a demon who attacked me, right?"

She nodded, then held herself back so she could look at him. "There's nothing to be sorry about. You are my mate, and I want to be where you are. Being banished to the mortal realm with you is no punishment. And we don't have to worry about the demons anymore. Ra made it so they would no longer be able to sense my presence since I can no longer be called on to protect mortals from them. We can be together." She brushed a kiss across his lips. "I love you, Cayden."

"I love you, Shesmetet. Forever."

As Cayden took Shesmetet's lips in a languid kiss, he vowed he'd show her every day that she was one gift he'd cherish for eternity.

The End

HIS SEA GODDESS

After a near miss with a shark while diving in the Red Sea in Egypt, Jarrett is rescued by a dolphin and unwillingly dragged to an underwater chamber. It isn't just any dolphin, though. Wounded and unsure of his surroundings, Jarrett watches in awe as it shifts into a beautiful woman he's unable to resist.

Hatmehyt, an Egyptian goddess, was drawn to the man swimming near the reef while in her dolphin form, but soon realizes Jarrett is her mate. Unable to thrive on land, she has to make the painful choice to either keep him with her or let him go to the surface when the shark bite he received threatens his life.

CHAPTER ONE

Jarrett Calder yanked open the curtains in his room at the Stella Grand Hotel in Ain Soukhna, Egypt, and peered out at the blue waters of the Red Sea. It looked to be a perfect day to get some diving in. Already a licensed diver, it was something he planned to do a lot of while on his vacation.

As he pulled on his swimsuit, Jarrett felt more of the tension—mostly caused by stress at work—leave him. Getting away for a week's vacation alone was just what he needed. His job as a stock broker at a large brokerage firm in Toronto, Canada, came with a lot of stress, especially now when the market had taken a turn for the worse. It'd been an ideal opportunity to get away. With no wife or girlfriend to take into consideration, it hadn't been too hard for Jarrett to take time off work and book one of those last-minute vacation deals.

Having already checked where to find the dive center at the hotel the evening before when he'd arrived, Jarrett knew exactly where to go to rent diving equipment. He had his day all planned. He'd swim out to the coral reef, then explore the sunken ships in the area for an hour, about as long as an A180 tank of compressed air would last. After that, he'd lay on the beach to work on his tan, and maybe hit the hotel's pool.

All geared up with scuba equipment, Jarrett waded into the sea. Once the water became deep enough, he pulled down his diving mask and stuck the regulator's mouthpiece into his mouth before he dove under the surface. Since the Red Sea was crystal clear, he had no problem seeing the multicolored fish and coral as he swam toward the reef.

Following it, Jarrett went farther from the shore. It grew deeper until he swam at a depth of almost thirty feet. With flicks of his flippers, he glided through the clear blue water, watching the fish swim in and out of the coral.

He spent the next fifteen minutes swimming around before deciding to go and look for the sunken ships. He hadn't gotten very far when a bull shark suddenly came out of nowhere. It swam by, butting Jarrett with his nose. His heart jumped into his throat as the large fish turned to make another pass. It had to be at least thirteen feet long. Not wanting to turn his back on it, he swam backward while he tried to put some distance between him and the shark, but it did little good. It rushed him with its jaws wide open. He in no way wanted to become a meal for this predator so when it came in reach, he punched it in the nose. He didn't get bit, but the shark's razor-sharp teeth grazed his lower leg at the calf when it swam past.

Jarrett looked down at his leg to find a tear in his wetsuit, as well as blood that seeped from it into the water. He clamped his hand over the wound. He gazed up. The shark was already circling back to make another run. He was screwed since he was too far from shore to call for help. He doubted anyone would be able to hear his yells even if he managed to make it to the surface in time. He was a good fifteen-minute swim from the beach.

Before the shark could get in range for a third time, a

streak of gray shot between him and it. Jarrett watched in amazement as a bottlenose dolphin rammed its nose into the shark's side. The dolphin continued to plough into the shark until it drove the predator away. In a different situation, he would have liked to stay and swim with the dolphin, but he was far from being out of danger. Other sharks would soon pick up the scent of his blood in the water. He turned his back on the dolphin and headed for shore.

*

In her dolphin form, Hatmehyt turned from the bull shark that she'd chased away to find the mortal she had saved trying to swim toward shore. Out for a swim around the coral reef, one of her favorite things to do, she'd spotted the man. She'd followed him at a discreet distance. Something about him had drawn her to him. It had nothing to do with his looks, because she had no idea what he really looked like covered up the way he was. He just appealed to her, making her want to be close to him. He intrigued her enough to have her doing what she normally avoided — interacting with a mortal.

She quickly swam after him. Even though his wound didn't seem to be bleeding too badly, it would be enough to draw every shark in the area. She went around in front of him and blocked his path. The only way he would survive without being attacked by another shark was for her to take him to her underwater home. It would be a much shorter swim than the one to the shore.

Once he stopped swimming, she swam up beside him and brushed her dorsal fin against his hand. As soon as he took hold, she towed him through the water in the opposite direction. No surprise, he let go once he realized they weren't headed for shore. Hatmehyt swam back to him and again positioned her dorsal fin under his hand.

This time he didn't take it. She debated whether or not to shift into her human form to show him she wasn't like the wild dolphins that lived in the area, but in the end she decided against it. It would only use up what little time they had left. So instead of offering her fin she gently took his wrist in her jaws and pulled him through the water.

Putting on a burst of speed, Hatmehyt didn't give the mortal a chance to resist. Determined to get him to her underwater home before anything else happened to him, she shot through the water. Once the underwater tunnel entrance came in sight, she let go of his wrist and used her nose to force him to swim through it.

She gave him another quick shove to keep him moving before she turned back to drive away another shark that had come up behind them. This one seemed more determined than the other as it came around for another pass. After a quick glance at the entrance to reassure herself that the mortal hadn't decided to come out, she focused her attention on the shark. It was time to teach this one what happened when you incurred the wrath of an Egyptian fish-goddess.

* * * *

Jarrett followed the long narrow tunnel the dolphin had shoved him into and soon noticed that up ahead it appeared to widen. Hoping it'd give him enough room to turn around so he could swim back out, he swam faster. He had no idea why the dolphin had taken him there, but he did know he couldn't stay. His air supply wouldn't last forever, and he had to get his leg looked at.

Once he reached the end of the tunnel, he saw he'd been right in his thinking. He found himself in what appeared to be an underwater cave. Looking above him, Jarrett saw the cave's ceiling hung high above the water. As he broke the surface of the small pool the cave had created, he removed his mouthpiece and sucked in a breath of fresh air. He treaded water, turning in place. What met his gaze made his mouth drop open.

This one could in no way be described as your typical underwater cave. The part that held the small pool was bare natural rock, but beyond that it gave way to a luxurious chamber. The walls had been painted in jewel tones with what appeared to be Egyptian hieroglyphs on top of that. Lit torches were interspersed along the walls, providing the only light. A large bed sat in the middle of the chamber with a canopy of sheer material that hung from the ceiling and down around the sides of it. Off to one side, a pile of thick pillows lay on the floor next to an unlit brazier. Shocked to find something such as this under the Red Sea, Jarrett slowly swam to the pool's edge.

Before he reached it, something brushed up against his leg. Thinking it could be another shark, he stiffened, but then relaxed when the dolphin broke the surface and made a series of clicks and then went to swim at his side. Once he reached the edge of the pool, Jarrett reached up and hauled himself out of the water. As soon as he sat on the ledge, he turned back just in time to see the dolphin's head appear on the surface. He blinked in surprise when its body shifted and blurred. Open-mouthed, he silently watched the dolphin disappear and a woman take its place. A beautiful naked woman who took his breath away.

Unable to tear his gaze off her, Jarrett ran it over her while she swam toward him. Her long, black hair fanned out behind her in the water as she glided nearer. Her brown-eyed gaze locked with his when she reached the side of the pool and then pulled herself out of the water to sit next to him. He gulped and pulled off his diving mask after she rose to stand. Starting at her feet, he skimmed her body with his gaze. She had long legs, curvy hips and full breasts. He lingered there while he took in her rose-colored nipples that had tightened into buds. His cock started to harden beneath his wetsuit. Moving higher, he stopped briefly on her full lips that looked as if they'd been made for a man to kiss before he moved on to the rest of her face.

She was drop-dead gorgeous. He tried to talk, but found his mouth had suddenly gone dry. Jarrett swallowed. "Who are you?"

She sank to her knees in front of him, totally at ease in her nakedness. "I am Hatmehyt. And who are you?"

Jarrett noted that Hatmehyt spoke in the same Egyptian-accented English as the workers at his hotel. She obviously had to be Egyptian, but that didn't explain how she was able to do the things she did. Right about now, he was starting to think all the stress at work had finally gotten to him.

He looked from her to the pool and back again. "I'm...I'm Jarrett. How is it possible you were a dolphin one minute then a woman the next? I don't think I've lost that much blood to cause me to hallucinate."

Hatmehyt gave him a small smile and shook her head. "You aren't hallucinating. I'm an Egyptian fish-goddess. I'm able to take on my dolphin form whenever I wish."

"You're an Egyptian goddess?" Jarrett asked with no small amount of incredulity as she reached for his injured leg.

Could he be dreaming? The Egyptian gods did not exist. Could they? Maybe he wasn't really there. Maybe the shark had ended up doing more damage and even now he was lying washed up on the beach slowly bleeding to death from a shark bite. When he felt the sting of his wound on his leg when Hatmehyt touched it, he knew he wasn't dreaming. She felt all too real.

"I can tell from your voice you don't believe I am what I say I am." She scowled and poked his wetsuit-clad leg. "If I'm to tend your wound properly I need this strange outer skin you wear removed."

Jarrett pulled off his flippers, then reached behind his back. He unzipped his wetsuit before he shrugged it from his shoulders and down his arms. He lifted his hips so he could push it the rest of the way off, leaving him in his swimsuit. He bit back a groan when he looked down at his lap. Now there would be no hiding the erection he had going on.

"Of course I find it hard to believe," he said. "It isn't as if I thought Egyptian gods actually existed."

She picked up his leg and placed his foot on her bare thigh while she bent over it to get a closer look at his wound. Jarrett had to bite the inside of his cheek to stop the moan that threatened to break free when the tip of Hatmehyt's breast brushed against his shin. He couldn't stop his body from reacting to her. He should be questioning his sanity, and instead, all he could think about was if he had a chance of getting her under him while he sank his cock inside her.

"Well, as you can see we are real," she said as she poked his leg.

Jarrett drew in a sharp breath between his teeth as Hatmehyt squeezed the sides of his wound. "I'd very much appreciate it if you didn't do that again."

She looked up and gave him an apologetic look. "Sorry. I really do need to clean it, though. You're lucky she didn't sink her teeth into you."

"She?"

"The shark. It was a female."

"Oh."

Jarrett really didn't care whether the shark that had almost taken a chunk out of him was male or female. To be honest, he didn't care too much about anything at the moment, except for the woman who knelt in front of him. The sight of her naked body made his blood heat. He had to fist his hands at his sides to stop himself from reaching for her. His cock throbbed in time with his heartbeat. All he could think about was how gorgeous Hatmehyt looked in all her naked glory, and how he wanted to explore every inch of her. He slid his gaze down to her pussy. He licked his lips, wondering how she'd taste.

He gave himself a mental shake. He sat bleeding from a shark bite while a supposed mythical Egyptian goddess tended it, and all he could think about was how soon he could have sex with her. He had to be losing it.

A bowl of water and a cloth appeared out of thin air next to Hatmehyt. She dipped the cloth into the water, then proceeded to clean his wound. Even though it stung, the small amount of pain did nothing to cool the heat of his body. If anything, the feel of her hands against his skin set him on fire. As arousal pounded through him, Jarrett couldn't deny the fact that he wanted her. He didn't care if she was a real Egyptian goddess or not. None of that seemed to matter. The fact that she aroused him to the point of pain just by being near him made it all seem irrelevant whether he believed her or not. He wanted her. No, he *needed* to have her.

With lust pounding through his veins, Jarrett reached out and circled her nipple with his fingertip. Hatmehyt's hands stilled, her gaze colliding with his. When she didn't push his finger away, he used his other hand to cup the back of her head. Slowly, to give her the chance to pull away, he brought her lips to his. She sighed against his mouth, and he knew he'd found bliss.

CHAPTER TWO

His mouth slanted over hers as Jarrett increased the pressure. She let her eyes drift shut on a sigh. Mindful of his wound, she braced her hands on his knee and leaned into the kiss. His tongue came out and swept the seam of her lips, and she opened. His tongue twined with hers, which caused the ache deep in her pussy to increase and wetness to pool between her legs. He sucked her tongue into his mouth while he cupped her breast and rubbed his thumb against her nipple. Waves of pleasure shot down to her core.

Hatmehyt kneeled between Jarrett's legs, placing her hands on his shoulders and leaning closer. His scent filled her head — a mixture of sea water and the musky scent of an aroused male. The smell of him excited her even more. It had been so long since she'd let a man inside her body. It craved his touch. She'd never slept with a mortal before, mostly because she hadn't found herself attracted to any, but that wasn't the case with Jarrett. She burned for him. The thought of his hard cock pumping inside her pussy made her heart race.

After pulling away, she looked at Jarrett and swept her

162

hands down his shoulders to his well-muscled chest. His hazel eyes stared back. He was an exceptionally good-looking man with his longish, sandy-blond hair and chiseled looks. She dropped her gaze and ran it over his muscled arms and stomach. She took her bottom lip between her teeth once she reached his erection. The short leg coverings he wore did nothing to hide the large bulge beneath them.

Hatmehyt stood and offered her hand to Jarrett. He took it, letting her help him stand. She wrapped her arm around his waist for support as she walked him to her bed. Her head just reached his shoulder. He was a tall man. He had to be well over six feet, and he was muscular as well.

Once they reached her bed, Hatmehyt helped him sit. Knowing where this would lead, she thought to offer to bandage his leg first, but that thought soon flew out of her mind. Jarrett reached for her, positioning her so she stood between his spread thighs. With his hands on her hips, he swirled his tongue around one of her nipples. Her breath caught as he flicked it with the tip before he sucked it inside his mouth. He suckled at her breast, and she threaded her fingers through his hair and pressed closer.

With each pull of his mouth, her pussy rippled with pleasure. "That feels good," she murmured on a scant breath.

A moan escaped her lips when Jarrett cupped her bottom and kneaded the twin globes of flesh. Wetness gathered between her legs to leak down the insides of her thighs as he switched his attention to her other breast. One of his hands left her bottom and came around to rest on her hip before he trailed his fingers down to her pussy. She tightened her grip on his hair while his fingers delved between the folds of her sex. As he stroked her clit, Hatmehyt moaned and jerked her hips.

Jarrett released her breast and looked at her when he pushed one finger inside her core. "You're so wet. I want to be inside you, but I want to taste you first."

He wrapped his arms around her waist and pulled her down onto the bed. Jarrett rolled her to her back and urged her to the middle of it. His lips claimed hers in a heated kiss while one of his thighs came to rest between her legs. Hatmehyt ground her pussy against it, moaning into his mouth.

Jarrett trailed kisses along her jaw and down to the side of her neck, licking and sucking the delicate flesh there before moving downward. Kissing the top of her shoulder, he undid the tie on his short leg coverings, then pushed them down past his hips and off. Hatmehyt reached down and wrapped her hand around his engorged cock, finding him thick and hard. She pumped up and down his length and rocked her hips against him. She couldn't wait to have him buried deep inside her.

With a groan, Jarrett pulled her hand off his cock. "That feels too good. If you keep that up, I'll come before I'm inside you."

Continuing his downward path, Jarrett headed to her breasts. He took the time to suck each of her nipples before he left them to trace his tongue down her ribs to her stomach. He flicked inside her bellybutton with his tongue as he shifted and settled between her legs. His breath tickled the inside of her thigh when he moved even lower.

She dug her fingers into the mattress at the first swipe of his tongue along her sex. Hatmehyt lifted her hips as he stroked her from bottom to top, then swirled around her clit. He lapped at her pussy while her moans filled the chamber. They increased in volume when Jarrett pushed one finger, then a second, inside her and pumped them in and out. He sucked on her clit, causing her body to coil even tighter. With her hands fisted in his hair, she pulled, trying to urge him back up.

Jarrett gave her pussy one last lick before he climbed up her body. Hatmehyt took hold of his cock and brushed the head of it against her. As he rocked his hips between her legs, she positioned him at her entrance and then pushed down. He surged inside her with one thrust, filling her to capacity. With his weight rested on his bent arms, he pulled back until he was almost free of her body only to push back inside. He hardened even more while he pumped his hips between her legs. The feel of his thick shaft stroking her clit with each thrust sent shockwaves of pleasure through her pussy.

Hatmehyt wrapped her legs around Jarrett's waist as he pumped into her harder, faster. The sound of their heavy breathing filled the chamber. With her strong inner walls clenched around his cock, she angled her hips, meeting each of his strokes. Going up on his hands, he lifted his upper body off her. He pounded into her while her climax inched closer, then she was there. She clutched his biceps as her body spasmed around his length, squeezing him in a tight fist. He threw back his head in a groan and stiffened above her, pulsing deep inside her as he came.

Jarrett collapsed on top her while they both fought to regain their breath. Hatmehyt held him tight. With her emotions in turmoil, she stroked his back. He was the one. He was her mate. As they had made love, she'd felt the mating bond form between them. His being her mate explained why her body burst into flames with the first brush of his hand, and why she'd been drawn to him in the first place. They had been fated to be together.

Hatmehyt was thrilled that she had finally found him, but taking Jarrett to be her mate would more than complicate her life. As a fish-goddess, she had never felt comfortable living on the surface, be it in the mortal or immortal realm. She felt more at home living in her undersea chamber, able to shape shift to her dolphin form and swim with the other animals of the sea. She didn't do well on land for any length of time.

Lifting some of his weight off her, Jarrett brushed her

lips with his. "That was amazing. You even managed to make me forget about my sore leg."

"Your leg," she exclaimed. "It needs to be bandaged."

She pushed at Jarrett's shoulder until he rolled onto his back. Hatmehyt gently turned his wounded leg toward her. It had started to bleed again. What kind of mate would she be if she couldn't even remember to take care of him when injured? She also had to remember he was mortal.

Her brows drew together as she thought of his mortality. Only a minor goddess, she didn't have the power to make him immortal. How could Jarrett be her true mate if she couldn't grant him immortality? The answer was simple—it would never be possible. Even though it hurt to think about it, she would have to give him up. They may have been destined to be mates, but she couldn't see how it could work. He couldn't survive under the water, and she could never thrive on land.

Jarrett cupped her cheek in his hand. "Hatmehyt? Is something the matter? You look kind of sad."

She shook her head. "It's nothing. Come. I have to clean your wound again. I'll do it over by the brazier."

They slipped off her bed and went to the mound of pillows on the floor next to the brazier. She waved toward it to light it. She also willed another bowl of warm fresh water, a clean cloth and a long strip of linen to use as a bandage. Jarrett limped noticeably when he walked. Hatmehyt got him to lay on the pillows while she dipped the cloth into the water and then squeezed out the excess. She wiped the wound and examined it closely. It didn't look as if it had started to become infected, at least not yet. He winced when she cleaned it and then wrapped the bandage around his leg.

"How did it look?" Jarrett asked as she secured it by tying the ends into a knot.

"It's fairly deep. You'll probably end up with a scar."

He smiled. "I don't mind. Whenever I look at it I'll be reminded of you."

Climbing onto the pillows next to him, she didn't say anything in response to his comment. The thought of him needing to be reminded of her didn't sit too well. When he left her, she wanted him to always remember their time spent together. To do that, she would have to convince him to stay with her, at least for a little while. The more they made love the closer their bond would become. It would hurt her to let him go, but she wanted the memories they would make there. She needed them since they would have to last her through the long, lonely centuries she would have to face without Jarrett.

She lay against his side with her head pillowed on his chest. Hatmehyt placed her hand over his heart, which beat strong and steady. "Stay with me, Jarrett."

"You want me to stay here with you?"

"Yes."

"I don't know if that would be such a good idea," Jarrett said slowly. "I don't live in Egypt. I'm only here on vacation, Hatmehyt. If I don't return to the hotel, the place where I'm staying, they're bound to notice I've gone missing. I'm sure the people at the dive center where I rented the diving equipment will be the first to mark my disappearance when I don't return it on time."

"I thought you would want to spend more time with me."

"I do." Jarrett put his hand under her chin and forced her to look up. "I do want to spend time with you. I've never been as attracted to a woman as I am to you. How about a compromise?" He gave her a sexy grin. "Why don't we spend the rest of the day, and the night, in my hotel room? I had planned to spend most of my vacation diving, but the idea of being in my room with you appeals to me more."

If only she could, but Hatmehyt wouldn't last an hour

on land before she became anxious to return to the water. "I can't, Jarrett. I would never survive being on land for that long."

"The beach is just outside my hotel room. You could always take a quick dip in the sea, then come back inside," he coaxed.

"You don't understand. It isn't that I *need* to be in the water to survive. I can't stay on the land. I just can't." Her last words came out sounding a bit desperate.

Jarrett moved her so she lay sprawled on top him. He cupped her face. "It's okay, Hatmehyt. I understand. It's more a mental thing than a physical. I get it."

"Then you know why I can't be with you at your hotel room."

"Yes." His gaze ran over her face. "I'm not ready to leave you. I can't explain it, but for some reason I *need* to be with you. I know we just met, and I really don't understand much about you, I can't for the life of me walk away."

Hatmehyt closed her eyes. Jarrett was feeling their mating bond as well. She wanted to tell him exactly why he felt the things he did, but she wouldn't. It would be better if he never learned they were mates.

She opened her eyes and gave him a small smile. "Then will you stay here with me?"

*

Jarrett brushed his thumb along Hatmehyt's full bottom lip. Should he stay? His body yelled hell yes, but his mind still hadn't decided. If not for the fact he was booked into a hotel that would notice his absence, and the fact that he'd gotten a chunk taken out of him by a shark, he would have had no reservations about staying. Even now his leg throbbed, but he didn't know if that was from infection setting in or from Hatymehyt cleaning it.

He looked at her and sighed. He couldn't leave. The thought of never seeing her again caused an ache in his chest. He wanted her, god how he wanted her. With her on top him like this, his cock had already started to rise to the occasion between them. Then there was the very real need he felt to be near Hatymehyt. He found it wasn't something he could so easily ignore.

"Fine, I'll stay. I'll probably have a lot to answer for when I do eventually go back to the hotel, but right now, I don't care."

Hatmehyt placed a kiss on his chin. "I'll take care of you." She placed a light kiss on his lips. "I promise." She kissed him again. "I can already feel you have need of me." With a little wiggle, she brushed against his cock.

"Mmm, I do need you. I have an ache only you can take away, the sooner the better." Jarrett brought his hands down to her ass and held her tight as he ground his erection against her.

"I think that can be arranged."

Their lips came together in a hard open-mouthed kiss. Jarrett pushed his tongue inside as he tasted her. The feel of her naked skin pressed against his pushed his arousal even higher. God, how he wanted this woman, this goddess. He couldn't seem to get enough of her. The more he kissed her, touched her, made love to her, the closer he felt to Hatmehyt. It was almost as if another part of them came together when they joined their bodies, bringing them closer.

While Hatmehyt sucked on his tongue, Jarrett urged her to straddle his thighs. Once she did, he reached between them until he found her pussy. Still wet from their earlier lovemaking, he drew some of the wetness out of her core with his finger and then swirled it around her clit. Her hips jerked as he plucked at the center of her pleasure. As she moaned into his mouth, he slipped two fingers inside her wet passage. He groaned at the feel of her strong inner walls squeezing down around them.

Jarrett released her mouth and urged her to move up higher. "You make me ache for you, Hatmehyt," he said with a moan.

Her hands came to rest on the pillows on either side of his head, supporting her upper body above him. With his fingers still buried deep inside her, he cupped a breast in his other hand. He took her nipple between his teeth and lightly tugged before he sucked it inside his mouth. She cried out when he pumped in and out while he drew hard on her nipple.

His cock hardened even more when she rode his fingers, matching his strokes. He pressed deeper into the pillows so he could watch Hatmehyt's face. She had her eyes closed with her lips slightly parted while she moved up and down. After he pulled his fingers out of her pussy, she opened her eyes and watched as he ran them along the length of his shaft, coating himself with her wetness. With her gaze locked on his hand, Jarrett fisted his cock and pumped it up and down. He sucked in a breath when she licked her lips.

Going up onto her knees, Hatmehyt positioned herself above his cock. Jarrett kept his hand fisted on the base of his erection while she slowly took the head of his shaft inside her pussy. He gritted his teeth as an intense wave of pleasure washed through him. She moved her hips in a circular motion. He arched his back off the pillows for her to take more of him, but she kept her legs locked, only allowing the head to move in and out.

Jarrett panted, fighting the need to sheath himself to the hilt inside her. Once he thought he couldn't take any more, Hatmehyt pulled his hand away and pushed down until she'd impaled herself on his full length. They moaned as she arched her back to take him even deeper. Knowing he wouldn't last very long, he took hold of her hips and pushed up into her, matching her strokes. She kept the pace slow and steady, drawing groans of pleasure from them.

On the verge of exploding, Jarrett reached between them where their bodies were joined. He stroked her clit. The sight of his cock moving in and out of her pussy almost made him come then and there. Determined to make her reach her pleasure first, he continued to stroke her as she rode him faster. Then, her inner walls fluttering, clamping down around him, she came. Jarrett lifted into her one final time and bellowed as he climaxed. He arched, almost lifting Hatmehyt off the pillows, filling her with his cum.

Once the last waves of pleasure receded, Jarrett pulled Hatmehyt down onto his chest, wrapping his arms around her. His eyes fluttered shut. Satiated and tired, he started to drift off to sleep. Before he completely succumbed, a single word echoed inside his head—mine. She was his. Somehow he'd have to find a way to keep her, because he didn't think he could ever give her up.

CHAPTER THREE

Hatmehyt stood beside the bed and watched Jarrett sleep. After he'd taken a short nap, they had made love again on the pillows. Before they had returned to the bed, she'd willed some food to her chamber. As a goddess, her body did not require food as his did. She hadn't known how arousing it could be to feed a mortal, especially when that mortal happened to be her mate. Having him eat from her hand while he licked any food that remained off her fingers turned out to be the most erotic thing she had ever done. And it wasn't that he just ate what she had given him. He purposely allowed some of it to fall on her body, which he then licked away. He'd soon had her flat on her back with his head between her thighs, eating her instead of the food she offered.

Just thinking about it made her legs quiver and her pussy ache. Jarrett stirred in his sleep. He grimaced and moved his injured leg under the sheet. Hatmehyt lifted it away to look at it. The bandage still covered the wound, but when she placed her hand over it, it felt warm. Too warm. It could only mean one thing—his wound was becoming infected. Not wanting to poke and prod at him while he slept, she moved the sheet back. She'd have to look at his wound again once he woke up.

She ran her gaze over his body and up to his handsome face. She'd originally thought she could easily send him on his way, even though they had bonded, but now she wasn't so certain. Her feelings for him were too strong. She didn't think she could go back to living alone in her chamber as she had. Despite knowing she risked falling in love with Jarrett because he was her mate, the one destined to be hers, Hatmehyt had foolishly thought she'd be able to keep her heart safe. She'd underestimated the mating bond. When Jarrett left, he would take her heart with him.

Her head awhirl with thoughts of what she should do about Jarrett, Hatmehyt climbed into the bed next to him. She cuddled against his side and lay down. Inside her mind she ran through all the possibilities of how she could keep him as hers. The first thing she had to do was to somehow convince one of the other gods to grant him immortality since she could not. The name of one god came to mind — Ra. She had shunned the other gods and goddesses for so long she doubted any but Ra would listen to her plea.

She thought about her inability to handle living on land. She would be willing to try to adjust for Jarrett if it meant they could be together, but she couldn't leave the sea completely. She couldn't give up her beloved Red Sea. He had said he'd come to Egypt on vacation. She wasn't sure exactly what that word meant, but she had no idea where his home was.

Feeling more confused about what she wanted to do than not, Hatmehyt closed her eyes. Jarrett groaned in his sleep, and a sense of unease shot down her spine. She had a feeling his leg would get much worse the longer he stayed in her underwater home. It made her wish she had the ability to heal wounds like some goddesses did. Unable to do anything for her mate, she snuggled closer and drifted off into a fitful sleep.

* * * *

Jarrett came awake with a start. At first, he didn't remember where he was, but when he looked around and saw the brightly painted hieroglyphs on the walls, the events of the day before came back to him in a rush. He turned to look at the spot next to him on the bed, hoping to find Hatmehyt still asleep, but her side was empty. A quick scan of the chamber revealed it was empty as well.

Knowing the only other place Hatmehyt could be was in the pool, he sat up. He sucked in a breath when a sharp pain shot through his wounded leg. He bent his knee and looked down at the cloth bandage she'd wrapped around his calf. As he untied the knot and then unwound it, he felt the heat that came off his skin from around the wound. Warning bells went off. That couldn't be good.

With the bandage removed, Jarrett saw his worry hadn't been unfounded. The area around the wound was swollen. The torn edges were red and angry-looking. As he lightly squeezed, puss seeped out, confirming his leg had become infected.

Jarrett swung it over the side of the bed and stood. Seeing his swimsuit lay on the floor at his feet, he picked it up and then carefully pulled it on. With most of his weight on his uninjured leg, he painfully limped to the pool. Hatmehyt wasn't there either. He sat on the edge while he thought over his options. He could either stay with her as he'd promised and think of a way to get rid of the infection himself, or he had to leave and have the doctor at the hotel look at it. Yes, the leg had become infected, but it didn't look too bad, at least he didn't think it did. He *could* give it another day and see how things went from there.

He dipped his other leg into the pool. Swirling the water around, he breathed in the sea salted air. Salt. Jarrett stilled as he thought about what filled it. Salt was known to disinfect wounds. Maybe if he gave his wounded leg a good soak in the sea water it would take some of the infection away. It would hurt like a bugger, but if it kept it from getting further infected, he figured it'd be well worth the pain.

Jarrett held his injured leg over the water and sucked in a couple deep breaths. He gripped the edge of the pool tightly with both hands and shoved it in before he could talk himself out of it. "Son of a bitch!" he yelled. It felt as if someone had taken a red hot poker to his wound and held it there.

He continued to swear a blue streak while he forced himself to keep his leg submerged. So focused on his pain, he didn't at first notice Hatmehyt enter the pool in her dolphin form. She broke the surface of the water next to him and shifted to human form.

"What are you doing, Jarrett? You look very pale."

Through gritted teeth, he said, "My leg is infected. I'm hoping the salt water will help get rid of it."

"Doesn't that hurt?"

"Yes. Very much."

Hatmehyt pulled herself out of the pool and then sat beside him. "Then take it out of the water."

Unable to take the pain anymore, Jarrett yanked his leg out and placed it on the side of the pool. He squeezed the wound. More puss came out along with a small amount of blood. Hatmehyt hovered over his leg. He noticed she now wore a tight-fitting sea-blue linen sheath dress, which barely covered the tops of her breasts. If not for the searing pain in his leg, he'd have pulled her to him to see how easy it'd be to get her out of it.

He met Hatmehyt's worried gaze. "It's going to be okay."

She shook her head. "What if the infection gets worse?"

"Then I'll have to return to the hotel."

Hatmehyt stood and reached for his hand. "Let me help you back to bed. You're probably hungry, and I should put a clean bandage on your leg as well."

Jarrett let her help him up. When she wrapped her arm around his waist, he put his around her slim shoulders. He couldn't help but notice how well she fit under his arm. He also couldn't help but notice how sad Hatmehyt had looked when he'd said he'd have to return to the hotel if the infection worsened.

Hoping to lighten her mood, he said, "I am hungry. Maybe you'd like to handfeed me again." He wiggled his eyebrows.

She gave him a half-smile as she led him to the bed. "Not this time."

"Ah, you're no fun."

"Maybe later, after you have eaten and rested and I've taken care of your leg."

He grunted as he sat down and pulled himself onto the middle of the bed. "I'm not tired. Maybe you'd like to kiss my leg better, as well as the rest of me."

A smile tugged at Hatmehyt's lips. After getting him to bend his knee, she placed his foot flat on the bed. "Would that take your pain away?"

"Most definitely."

"We shall see then."

While she worked, Jarrett asked, "Where were you?"

"I went for a swim near the reef."

He watched Hatmehyt meet his gaze before she quickly looked away. "And?"

She sighed. "There were other mortals swimming at there. They were dressed in the same strange outer skin you wore. They appeared to be looking for something."

So the hotel had already sent out a search party. When they didn't find his body, which he presumed they were looking for, they'd contact his next of kin in Canada. Luckily for him, or not, depending on how you wanted to look at it, his only family was his older brother whom he hadn't spoken to in over eight years. The last time he'd seen him had been at their mother's funeral. As for his father, he'd taken off when Jarrett had been five, and they hadn't heard from him since.

"They're looking for me," he said softly.

"I know."

Hatmehyt seemed to withdraw into herself. As she tied the last knot on his bandage, Jarrett pulled her up beside him. He tipped her chin. "Look at me, Hatmehyt. I'm not going to leave just because they've already started to search for me. I promised I'd stay. To be honest, I don't think I can leave you now. Ridiculous as this may sound, it'd be as if I left a piece of myself behind. I never thought of myself as the type of man able to fall in love so quickly, but I think I love you, Hatmehyt."

Having worked up the courage to make his declaration of love to Hatmehyt, Jarrett watched with dismay when she got off the bed and stood with her back toward him. He flopped back and threw an arm over his eyes. Now he'd gone and done it. He should have kept his mouth shut, but he'd been so sure she felt the same way he did. He was an idiot. Did he really think an immortal Egyptian goddess could ever love a mortal? Not wanting her to kick him out when he wasn't ready yet to leave he opened his mouth to do some back peddling.

Before he could say anything Hatmehyt turned back around, and whispered, "I love you, too."

Jarrett sat up. "What did you just say?"

"I said I love you."

For someone who'd just professed her love, Hatmehyt didn't look overjoyed about it. "But?"

Hatmehyt shifted from one foot to the other. "How old are you, Jarrett?"

He blinked at the sudden change in topic. "I'm thirty-two. What does that have to do with you loving me?"

She wrapped her arms across her stomach. "You're mortal."

"I'm very aware of that fact."

Hatmehyt took a deep breath and then said in a rush, "We are mates. That's why we fell in love so quickly. I can't give you immortality like some other goddesses. If I had that ability, we could have the forever together that we're meant to have. I'm willing to try to live on the surface with you, but I won't leave the Red Sea. I won't leave Egypt. Even then I don't know if I'll be strong enough to stay on land."

Jarrett inched to the edge of the bed and put his feet on the floor. He tugged Hatmehyt onto his lap. "Whoa, slow down. Let's take it one step at a time. Okay?" She nodded, and he asked, "So we're mates?"

"Yes. I knew it the first time we made love and the mating bond formed between us. That's why we don't want to be separated from each other."

Hearing her tell him they were mates sent a thrill through Jarrett. It also made him feel better to know he wasn't losing it, that what he felt for her was indeed real. If they were mates, then he didn't have to give her up and Hatmehyt could be his.

His thoughts went to the second part of what she'd said. "Now what is this about some goddesses being able to give mortals immortality?"

"They have the power to turn their mortal mates immortal. I'm only a minor goddess so my powers aren't as strong as others. They have more to do with the creatures of the sea. If I had such a power, I would have asked you right from the start to be my mate."

Jarrett brought her lips down to his and gave her a light kiss. That Hatmehyt would have offered him immortality if she were able sent a warm feeling washing through him. "I would have said yes. And if it were possible, I would want forever with you too."

"There may still be a way to give us that."

"How?"

"I would have to contact Ra and ask him to grant you immortality."

"Ra is the ruler of the Egyptian gods?"

"Yes. I could ask some of the other gods or goddesses to help us, but I've kept to myself for so long I doubt any of them except for Ra would."

"Then ask him."

"And if he says he will do it? What then? You would have to give up everything to be with me. Your home. Your family."

He chuckled. "That wouldn't be much of a hardship, Hatmehyt. I wouldn't mind not going back to Canada. I know I won't miss the cold, snowy winters. I really don't have much in the way of family, just an older brother who hates my guts and whom I never see. I have a good chunk of money saved. I think it'd be enough to buy us a secluded place on the beach. I'm willing to do whatever it takes to keep you."

"And if it works out I can't stay on land?"

"Then we'll split our time between our house on the land and your underwater chamber. We can make this work."

"You would be willing to do all that for me?" she asked softly.

"Of course. That's what people in love do, isn't it? They willingly make changes in their lives so they can live with the one they love."

With a small cry, Hatmehyt leaned against him and brought her mouth down onto his. Jarrett fell back with her in his arms as she plunged her tongue past his lips. While she swept the inside of his mouth, she shifted until she was on her hands and knees above him. He used his elbows to pull himself to the center of the bed. She followed, keeping her lips locked with his. Now that they knew how they felt for each other, his need for her pounded swiftly through him.

The pain in his leg forgotten, he kissed her back with all the love he felt. Angling his lips across hers, he increased the pressure of his mouth. Hatmehyt moaned as he sucked on her tongue, the sound causing his cock to grow hard inside his swimsuit. She would always have this effect on him. No matter how many times he took her, he'd want more.

He ran his hands down the sides and back of her dress, searching for a zipper or some kind of fastener so he could undo it and slip it off. When he didn't find any kind, he said against her lips, "Tell me how to get this off you."

She took his bottom lip between her teeth and tugged before she answered. "Like this."

A wave and Hatmehyt's dress disappeared. With another, Jarrett found himself equally naked. "That is one power I wish I had," he said before he claimed her lips once again.

Hatmehyt's mouth left his and trailed to his chin. She nipped him there before she dragged her tongue down his throat to his chest. His cock jerked when she licked his nipple before she took the small nub between her teeth. Jarrett couldn't hold back a moan of pleasure as she did the same to his other one.

He lifted his head off the mattress to watch her make her way down his abs. He groaned when she brought her mouth level with his fully erect cock. She licked her lips, then used a finger to rub the bead of pre-cum that sat on the very tip into his skin. All the blood in his body seemed to rush to his erection as she wrapped her hand around his shaft and licked him from base to tip. The sight of her tongue swirling around the head made him lift his hips toward her. Once she opened her mouth and finally took him inside, Jarrett let his head fall back. He closed his eyes and focused on the pleasurable sensations that swept through him while she sucked him.

The feel of her sucking, taking as much as she could manage inside her mouth, made his cock harden painfully. Unable to control himself, Jarrett rocked his hips and pushed more of his length past her lips. It was almost too much. As if she sensed it wouldn't take much to send him into an orgasm, Hatmehyt gave him a last lick before she moved up his body. He opened his eyes, grabbed her around the waist and flipped her onto her back. He bit back a groan when he felt a painful pulling sensation on his wound. Pushing the pain away, he positioned himself between her legs and sheathed himself to the hilt with one hard thrust.

He cupped her ass and lifted her hips as he pounded into her. Hatmehyt wrapped her legs around his waist, clamping her inner muscles around his shaft. Jarrett rode her hard and fast all the while his climax edged nearer. From the small sounds she made as he thrust, he knew it wouldn't be long before she too found her release. Increasing his pace, he slammed into her. Her legs tightened once she fell over the edge. She let loose with a keening moan. Her pussy squeezed his cock in a tight fist while she came. He pushed into her one final time and emptied deep inside her core.

Jarrett collapsed on top Hatmehyt and kissed the side of her neck. His leg throbbed painfully, but he ignored it. He kept their bodies joined and rolled them to their sides with her leg over his hip.

Once he could breathe normally again, he asked, "So when do you want to try to contact Ra?"

"You truly want to be my mate?"

He rolled his eyes. "Of course I do. I want to have forever with you as well. I love you." He flexed his hips. "Do I have to show you again how much you mean to me?"

She smiled. "Yes, but I don't think you're quite up to

the job yet."

Jarrett cringed. "Now that's harsh. Give me a minute and I'll show you exactly how *up* I am for the job."

Hatmehyt squeezed her inner muscles around his semi-hard cock. "I can feel there is potential, but I think I'll get you something to eat first. You'll need to keep your strength up, along with other things."

He kissed the tip of her nose. "We definitely don't want me to get weak, and food is exactly what I need. I'm thinking seafood this time. Some lobster, fresh fish and most definitely some oysters to keep my stamina going."

She kissed his cheek before she leapt out of bed. "That can be arranged. And I won't have to use my powers to get them. I'll catch them for you myself."

Before Jarrett could say anything more, Hatmehyt ran to the pool and then dove in. Once she surfaced, she'd already shifted into her dolphin form. With a flick of her tail, she dove under the water once more and disappeared.

Jarrett smiled and shook his head. It was a good thing he liked the water as much as Hatmehyt. Now alone, he pulled his injured leg closer and looked at the bandage. A fair sized patch of blood discolored it. He probably had reopened the wound while he'd made love to her. The blood proved it. He pulled the sheet up to cover his injured leg and hips. He couldn't let her see it. It'd only make her worry even more. He'd just have to keep her mind on more pleasurable things to distract her.

CHAPTER FOUR

Hatmehyt returned to her chamber to find Jarrett snoozing. She woke him up with a kiss, then proudly showed him the large lobster she'd managed to catch. Along with it, she had also found six oysters. He had given her a kiss for each one of her catches.

The oysters and lobster, which she had cooked over the brazier, Jarrett ate with relish. After his meal, she decided to give him a bath since going into the pool with his wound would only cause him more pain. Willing a large bowl of fresh warm water, a scented bar of soap and a cloth at the side of the bed, she proceeded to bathe him. She had planned to wash his hair as well, but they never made it that far. She'd barely finished washing his body before he'd had her under him as he joined their bodies.

They ended up making love for most of the day. In between bouts of mind-blowing sex they talked. Jarrett spoke of his life in Canada, and about his mother who had died. His brother, Hatmehyt couldn't blame Jarrett for not wanting anything to do with him. As he'd said, his brother seemed to be no big loss. She told him stories about Egypt of old, and about how the gods used to walk among the mortals who had once worshipped them.

Once night fell, she'd snuggled beside Jarrett and slept. She'd only been asleep for an hour when she was awoken by his moans. With a wave, she relit the torches on the wall closest to the bed. Hatmehyt lifted herself onto one elbow and stared down at her mate. His cheeks were unnaturally flushed. Waves of heat rolled off his body, even though his teeth chattered while he shivered. Placing her palm on his forehead, she found it hot to the touch. A chill ran down her spine. She'd once seen a mortal die from such a fever after being wounded in battle.

Scared at what she would find, Hatmehyt pulled the sheet away from Jarrett's injured leg. She swallowed when she saw the large patch of blood that marred the bandage's pristine whiteness. Quickly undoing the knots, she tried to unwind it, but the bandage had dried to the wound. She'd do more damage if she just pulled it off. She slipped off the bed and willed a dress on her body. She went to Jarrett's side and gently shook his shoulder.

"Jarrett, wake up."

He blinked at her with fever-bright eyes. "I'm cold."

"I know. I have to soak the bandage off your leg. It may hurt. I think you have wound fever, but I don't know what to do to help you."

His teeth chattered when he spoke. "We...need to bring...the fever down. Cold...water."

Hatmehyt pulled the sheets up to Jarrett's chin and then willed a large bowl of cold water to her side. When a cloth appeared in her hand, she dipped it in and then wrung it out before she folded it and placed it on his forehead. With another cloth, she soaked the bandage from his leg. He moaned with pain once she was able to pull it free. Her heart dropped at the sight of the festering wound. Puss ran from it when she gently probed.

For the remainder of the night she bathed Jarrett's

forehead with cold water, hoping it would bring down his fever. It didn't work. While dawn broke on the surface, he thrashed on the bed as it spiked even higher.

Knowing if she didn't do something soon he would die, Hatmehyt couldn't hold off contacting Ra any longer. With Jarrett's hand held in hers, she focused inside herself and called out to the ruler of the Egyptian gods. "Ra, hear me," she said out loud. "I have need of you. My mate is very ill. I ask that you grant him immortality. He already gave his consent before falling ill. Please do for him what I can't."

She fell silent and waited to hear Ra's response, but no answer came.

With tears streaming down her face, Hatmehyt tried one more time. "I beg of you, Ra. Please save my mate."

When she still didn't get a response, she closed her eyes and sank to the floor next to the bed. Ra hadn't listened to her plea. A sob rose in her throat. For some reason, Ra had forsaken her. If he wouldn't help her in her time of need, what were the chances that he would listen to her at all?

Jarrett said something unintelligible as he thrashed again. Wiping her tears away, Hatmehyt knew she only had one option left if she were to save his life. She pulled the sheet off him and willed his short leg coverings back on his body. She willed on the strange outer skin he'd worn out in the water. That done she somehow managed to get him out of the bed and then into her pool. Next she willed the heavy metal tank onto his back along with the mask he'd worn and the fins on his feet. Before she shifted to her dolphin form, she gave him one last kiss before she put the tank's mouthpiece into his mouth.

With Jarrett's wrist in her jaws, Hatmehyt towed him through the underwater entrance and then out into the open sea. As she swam toward shore, she hoped she picked the right beach, and that someone would find him quickly. Once the water became too shallow for her to swim in as a dolphin, she shifted to her human form and dragged him up onto the beach. She looked toward the large building that sat not too far from the water. There appeared to be a few people milling about in the distance. Someone would spot him there, she hoped.

Not wanting to be seen, Hatmehyt quickly pulled the tank off Jarrett's back and took the mouthpiece out of his mouth before she rolled him onto his back on the sand. She kissed him again, then whispered, "I love you. I'll never forget you." Telling herself this was the only way, she ran back into the sea.

* * * *

Jarrett came slowly awake with someone shaking his shoulder. He fought to open his eyes when all he wanted to do was go back to sleep.

"Wake up now, Mr. Calder. I need you to wake up."

He blinked several times until the face of a man came into focus. "Where am I?"

The man smiled. "You're in the hospital."

Jarrett had no recollection of ending up in a hospital. The last thing he remembered was being with... "Hatmehyt," he said out loud.

"No," the man said. "I'm Dr. Hassan. You're one lucky man, Mr. Calder. The shark bite you received was a nasty one. I'm happy to say we were able to save your leg and surgically remove the infection."

He listened to the doctor with half an ear. Hatmehyt must have taken him to the surface when his fever had worsened. Why hadn't she stayed? He needed to get back to her, to let her know he'd be all right.

He tried to sit up, but the doctor easily pushed him back down. "I need to leave."

The doctor shook his head. "You're not going anywhere for the next couple days. You still need to be given antibiotics to ensure the infection doesn't come back. What do you remember about what happened? You were missing for two days."

Jarrett looked down at his arm where a thin tube ran from the top of his hand to an IV drip. He shook his head. "A bull shark attacked me, but a dolphin came and drove it away. After that..." He let his words fall away. He wasn't about to tell the doctor anything about his time spent with Hatmehyt. For one thing the doctor would think he'd lost his mind if he started talking about the Egyptian goddess who'd saved him and who lived in a nearby undersea chamber. "How was I found?"

The doctor smiled. "It's normal when a person goes through a traumatic experience to have their mind block some of it. One of the staff at your hotel found you unconscious on the beach just after dawn."

So Hatmehyt had to have taken him to the beach. She must have thought returning him to the surface would be the only way to save him. She also must be worried sick about him. It made the need to return to her that much stronger. "How long have I been here?"

"Three days."

"Three days?" he asked with disbelief.

"You've been very sick, Mr. Calder. I know you're anxious to leave the hospital, and that you're scheduled to return to Canada in a couple days. I strongly suggest you use the remainder of your stay here to rest and recuperate. I'll come by later this evening to check in on you before I leave for the day."

Jarrett nodded absentmindedly. Three days. He'd been in the hospital for three days already with at least another two to go. Did Hatmehyt think he was dead? She could since he'd yet to return to her. It chaffed being stuck in the hospital when all he wanted was to be with her. Knowing he couldn't do anything about it, he relaxed against the pillows on the bed. Right now he felt as weak as a kitten. Determined to change that as fast as he possibly could, he closed his eyes and let the lethargy he suddenly felt overtake him.

* * * *

Jarrett put his last two days in the hospital to good use. In between sleeping and eating, he set plans into motion for his immigration to Egypt. The first thing he did was call his work to tell them he'd been injured and that he'd return to Canada when he could. He didn't want to resign from his job over the phone.

His leg, still sore, slowly started to heal. Even though he'd been ordered by the doctor to keep off it as much as possible, Jarrett took every opportunity he could to exercise it. He limped around his hospital room until it throbbed. He needed it to be stronger to make the swim back to Hatymehyt's underwater chamber.

On the morning he was to be released, Jarrett sat on his bed impatiently waiting for his doctor to come see him one last time. After the doctor okayed him to leave, he'd head to his hotel, which he'd arranged to stay at for another week.

Dr. Hassan didn't keep him waiting long. He changed the dressing on Jarrett's leg before he gave him some last-minute instructions. "Keep the wound covered for the next couple days, then you can remove the bandage. And be sure to keep it dry, even in the shower."

"So going swimming in the sea is out?" Jarrett asked.

"I wouldn't recommend it," the doctor said with a smile. "I've already signed the forms for your release so you can leave any time. Come back to the hospital if it looks as if the infection has returned. Other than that, I hope you enjoy the rest of your vacation."

Jarrett couldn't get out of the hospital fast enough. The taxi ride to his hotel seemed to take forever. Thoughts of Hatmehyt bounced around inside his mind. He couldn't wait to see her again. She'd never strayed far from his thoughts the whole time he'd been stuck in the hospital. He'd even dreamed about her at night, of taking her into his arms as he made love to her. Each morning he woke up with his cock hard and achy.

On the way up to his hotel room, he stopped at the gift shop and asked for some of their plastic bags. He also bought a roll of thick clear packing tape. Once up in his room, he didn't waste any time changing into his swimsuit. He cut up one of the plastic bags and wrapped it around his leg before he used the packing tape to secure it to his skin. Satisfied it should keep his wound dry under a wetsuit, he headed out to the dive center.

It took more than a little convincing on his part to get the guy to allow him to rent the equipment he wanted, but in the end Jarrett prevailed. Suited up and ready to go, he headed for the beach and then out into the water.

Jarrett swam to the coral reef. This time he kept his eye out for any sharks that might be in the area. Once he arrived at the reef, he headed in what he thought was the direction of the underwater entrance to Hatmehyt's chamber. After twenty minutes of searching and he still hadn't found it, he realized he didn't really know where it was. He'd gotten pretty turned around on the day the shark had attacked him and then he'd been too worried about where the dolphin was taking him to pay too much attention to his surroundings.

Not daunted in the least, Jarrett continued to search for the tunnel. It had to be near there somewhere. He also kept an eye out for any dolphins, hoping Hatmehyt would find him while she swam in her dolphin form.

When minutes turned into an hour, he questioned whether he'd be able to find the entrance at all. Still unable to give up the search, Jarrett swam in and around the coral reef until he could hardly move his wounded leg and he'd almost run out of air. He limped back to the dive center and then arranged to go back out after he'd had some food and water.

As Jarrett ate his lunch inside his hotel room, he tried not to think about what he'd do if he couldn't find Hatmehyt. He shook his head. He wouldn't allow thoughts like that to get the better of him. He *would* find her. If only there was something or someone who could point him in the right direction. For some reason, that thought brought Ra's name to mind. Jarrett, not one for turning to a higher power in his time of need, wondered if he called Ra would he get an answer in return. At this point, he was willing to try anything.

He cleared his throat before he talked to the room at large. "Ra, I don't know if you can hear me, I really do need your help. Help me find Hatmehyt. Help me to return to my mate. I don't care if you grant me immortality or not. I just want to share what I have left of my life with Hatmehyt."

Jarrett fell silent. As he'd expected, no godly voice answered his plea. He snorted. Of course Ra wouldn't answer. Why would he? Mortals didn't believe he even existed so why would Ra take the time to listen to one such as him.

After he gave his food some time to digest, Jarrett headed back out to the beach. His injured leg ached abominably, but he wouldn't give up in his search for Hatmehyt's chamber. They were mates, and he wasn't going to let a little thing like his not knowing where to find it keep them apart.

Clad in a wetsuit, Jarrett carried his air tank over one shoulder and his fins in one hand as he limped his way to a less-used part of the beach. He had enough daylight left that if he didn't find the cave with this tank of air he could try again. It'd wear him out and have him risking the chance of the infection returning, but he'd count it as well worth it if the pain paid off in the end.

Deep in thought, thinking about where he'd start his search once he reached the reef, Jarrett at first didn't hear the small splashing sounds of someone coming out of the surf. Hearing a feminine gasp, he looked up to find Hatmehyt standing at the water's edge dressed in her sheath dress, staring at him with a sheen of unshed tears in her eyes. Dropping the fins and letting the tank slide off his shoulder to the sand, he opened his arms.

With a small cry, Hatmehyt threw herself into his embrace. "Jarrett, you're alive."

"You didn't think you'd get rid of me that easily, did you?" He said in a shocked voice, "You're on land."

Hatmehyt gave him a watery smile. "When I returned you to the surface, I thought I would be able to give you up, but I couldn't do it. The not knowing if you lived or not was a constant ache inside me. I decided I had to find out what your fate had been. For you, I planned to go to the hotel and search for you, stay on land for as long it would take for me to find you."

"You said you couldn't thrive on land."

"It would have been hard. It was also something I was willing to endure for you."

Jarrett took her mouth in a heated kiss. That Hatmehyt would go through that for him meant the world to him. It also meant she truly loved him. Lifting his head, he said, "I missed you, Hatmehyt. Returning to you was all I could think about while I was stuck in the hospital. That you would come to the surface tells me more than words ever could that you love me as much as I love you. Now that we've found each other, there isn't any reason for you to suffer. We'll work you gradually into spending more time on land with me. How about we go to your underwater chamber?"

She smiled sweetly at him. "Are you sure?"

"Yes. Let's get out of here."

Jarrett donned his flippers and then put the air tank

onto his back. With his mask pulled over his eyes and nose, the regulator in his mouth, he followed Hatmehyt into the water. Holding on to her dorsal fin, she towed him through the water to her underwater home. Once they reached the pool, she shifted to her human form while he pulled himself up onto the ledge. It didn't take him very long to take off his diving gear. By the time he'd removed it all Hatmehyt had joined him to stand at his side. Needing to be close, he pulled her into his embrace.

Before either of them could say anything, a loud male voice filled the chamber. "Hatmehyt."

Hatmehyt stiffened in Jarrett's arms. "Yes, Ra."

"I have returned your mate. He is worthy as the mate of a goddess. He did not give up his search for you. You proved yourself by being willing to endure something you weren't comfortable with for him. Is there something you would ask of me?"

"Yes." Hatmehyt swallowed. "I would ask that you give Jarrett, my mate, immortality so we may be together always."

"It shall be as you ask."

Jarrett sucked in a breath when a surge of power shot through him. It seemed to only last seconds, but it felt as if it'd shot through every cell in his body. The throbbing in his wounded leg disappeared, and he felt as if he could run a marathon.

He locked gazes with Hatmheyt as it receded as suddenly as it'd come. "I feel different. Stronger, better." He smiled. "My leg doesn't hurt anymore."

He sat on the bed, and when he tried to pull the packing tape off his leg, Hatmehyt went down on her knees and pushed his hand away. In a blink of an eye the plastic and bandage beneath it disappeared. Jarrett ran his hand up and down his leg. His wound was gone. Not even a scar marred his skin. No sign of the stitches that had been there seconds before showed. His leg looked as if the wound had never been.

He looked at Hatmehyt. "I'm immortal now."

She launched herself at him again. The momentum caused them to fall back onto the bed. Her mouth landed on his a second later. As he pushed his tongue inside her mouth, his cock hardened between them. He groaned when his swimsuit and Hatmehyt's dress disappeared.

Knowing they were now truly mates, Jarrett kissed Hatmehyt with all the love he felt. As she rose above him and then sheathed his cock inside her, he knew nothing would ever separate them again. He was home. No matter where they lived, on the land or inside this underwater chamber, as long as he had her at his side, it didn't matter. All that did was that they had each other, for now and the eternity to come.

The End

ABOUT THE AUTHOR

Marisa Chenery was always a lover of books, but after reading her first historical romance novel she found herself hooked. Having inherited a love for the written word, she soon started writing her own novels.

She now writes young adult books and erotic romances.

Marisa lives in Ontario, Canada, with her boyfriend, Steve, four children, four grandchildren (she's a young grandma in her fifties) and rabbit and dog.

www.marisachenery.com